PIECES OF WHY

K.L. GOING

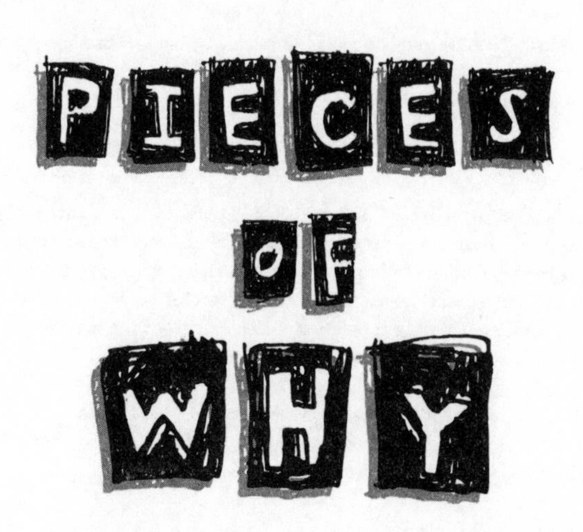

Kathy Dawson Books
an imprint of Penguin Group (USA) LLC

KATHY DAWSON BOOKS
Published by the Penguin Group
Penguin Group (USA) LLC
375 Hudson Street
New York, New York 10014

USA/Canada/UK/Ireland/Australia/New Zealand/India/South Africa/China
penguin.com
A Penguin Random House Company

Library of Congress Cataloging-in-Publication Data
Going, K. L. (Kelly L.), author.
Pieces of why / by K.L. Going.
pages cm
Summary: Twelve-year-old Tia lives in a white slum in New Orleans with her mother, and her whole world revolves around singing in the gospel choir with her best friend, Keisha—but when practice is interrupted by a shooting outside the church, and a baby is killed, Tia finds that she cannot sing, and she is forced to confront her feelings about her incarcerated father, who killed a girl in a failed robbery years before.
ISBN 978-0-8037-3474-6 (hardcover)
1. Gospel singers—Juvenile fiction. 2. Children's choirs—Juvenile fiction. 3. Children of prisoners—Juvenile fiction. 4. Traumatic neuroses—Juvenile fiction. 5. Fathers and daughters—Juvenile fiction. 6. Mothers and daughters—Juvenile fiction. 7. New Orleans (La.)—Juvenile fiction. [1. Gospel singers—Fiction. 2. Choirs—Fiction. 3. Traumatic neuroses—Fiction. 4. Fathers and daughters—Fiction. 5. Mothers and daughters—Fiction. 6. New Orleans (La.)—Fiction.] I. Title.
PZ7.G559118Pi 2015 813.6—dc23 [Fic] 2014040314

Printed in the United States of America
1 3 5 7 9 10 8 6 4 2

Designed by Nancy R. Leo-Kelly
Text set in Sentinel

For the 2.7 million children in the United States
with parents incarcerated, and for the baby

PIECES OF WHY

CHAPTER 1

CERTAIN DAYS ought to come with warning notices. **WARNING: This day will be hazardous to your health.** Instead, most days start out normal. Maybe even better than normal.

Which is so much worse.

~

I woke up feeling good. It was Thursday, and that meant choir practice. More than anything, I wanted to be a great singer. Not a rock star, but a singer who'd change the world with my voice, like Nina Simone, Whitney Houston, Adele, or Mahalia Jackson. I wanted my music to make people stop in their tracks.

Of course, seeing as I was only twelve and poor as dirt, that was a universe away, but if my voice teacher, Ms. Marion, had taught me anything, it was that even the most unlikely person could succeed.

"Didn't the great Mahalia grow up in a house right here in New Orleans with thirteen people under one roof?" she said. "Didn't she have to leave school in the fourth grade because her family couldn't afford to send her anymore? If a black girl could rise up in the early 1900s when everything was against her, then a skinny little white girl like you hasn't got any excuse."

So I kept one of those tear-off calendars beside my bed and the last thing I did every night was to rip off that day's page. It was a dumb calendar with facts about cars from a box of leftovers Ma hadn't been able to sell online, but that hardly mattered. All I wanted was the pleasure of crumpling up every day of the week that wasn't Thursday.

I sat up that morning and ran my fingers through my thick, tangled hair, and then I started a hum to warm up my vocal cords. Ms. Marion was a stickler about warming up properly.

Lazy singers never last.

Through the security bars on my window, I could see that the sky was full of clouds, ready to burst. The ominous streaks of gray might have been a sign, except in New Orleans storms can come and go in ten minutes flat—especially in June.

I got up and made my way into the shower, turning the water up hot and letting the spray scald my skin as I belted out the lead line of the gospel song my choir was practicing.

The Rainbow Choir was a chorus of kids made up of every race, color, and creed, and we were supposed to inspire a sense of community in our audiences. At least, that was Ms. Marion's vision. Me and my best friend, Keisha, had been founding members back when we were nine, but in the past three years, I wasn't sure we'd done any inspiring.

Still gave me an excuse to sing.

Ma and I lived in a rickety old shotgun house outside the Irish Channel. Our rooms were close together, so I was thankful Ma slept like the dead. Nothing woke her up—not even my powerful alto voice—so I could sing as loud as I wanted and let the acoustics in the bathroom carry the sound up to the ceiling.

I stepped out of the shower onto the gritty bare floor. New Orleans is hot as blazes in the summer, and I already felt sticky again—not a good sign this early in the day. I wished for the thousandth time that we had air-conditioning, but I propped open the bathroom window instead, hoping a breeze might come my way.

Nothing moved, outside or in.

I dressed, brushed my teeth, then pushed past the clutter to my bedroom. Ma's main job was as a baker at the Winn-Dixie on Tchoupitoulas, but as a side job she sold people's unwanted stuff online, and that meant our house was always chock-full of empty boxes, bubble wrap, foam peanuts, and random items like angel figurines, antique toys, or prom dresses that had gone out of style. Ma figured out how much they were worth, put them up for auction, and if they sold, she got a percentage. If the stuff didn't sell, half the time it ended up staying here.

Ma's bedroom is at the end of the house, so I had to step over a dozen puzzles and dusty Xbox games in order to peek inside. She was asleep on the oversized bed, and her uniform from the previous night's late shift had been dropped where she'd taken it off. A McDonald's hamburger wrapper and half a tub of fries lay on a chair where several small cockroaches were feasting on the remains.

Cockroaches gave me the creeps, so I set Ma's garbage pail next to the chair and took out our shoe-on-a-stick, then quickly pushed the whole mess into the bin before the cockroaches could scamper away. I tied up the garbage bag extra tight, wanting to retch, but I choked the feeling down.

For a moment, I stood watching Ma's thin frame rise and fall with sleep. Ma looked peaceful with her auburn hair spread loose across her pillow, but she'd had more than her share of troubles, and if anything else came her way, I suspected she'd crumble like the plaster on the stairs of the New Heaven Baptist Church. Those steps had looked fine, right up until two giant slabs fell off the side, revealing the twisted metal bars underneath.

I covered Ma with a blanket and kissed her cheek, then

went outside to practice my vocal exercises on the front stoop, knowing it would be a long wait for choir.

I was right. It took half of forever and a quarter of eternity.

What I didn't know was that the whole time I was waiting, trouble was creeping up, and it was the kind of trouble that would leave me and Ma swirling in its wake.

CHAPTER 2

ALL AFTERNOON, the temperature rose until the sidewalks steamed and the air was so still, I could barely breathe. I wasn't allowed to leave for choir practice until Ma woke up and we spent some time together, but that meant I waited around all day only to scrape by and barely make it to rehearsal before Ms. Marion called everyone onto the risers.

When Ma finally emerged from her bedroom dressed in her store uniform, my hair was damp against my forehead and frizzy from the humidity, and my patience had worn thin. I was sitting at the kitchen table eating a bowl of Apple Puffs with apple juice instead of milk because Ms. Marion says milk coats the vocal cords, making it difficult to sing.

"That is just plain gross," Ma said, leaning down to plant a kiss on the top of my head.

I shrugged. Wasn't that bad—the apple juice made the cereal tart against my tongue. "I have choir tonight," I reminded her.

She glanced at the clock. "You think I don't know that?"

"And . . . tomorrow night is June Fest," I mumbled, studying the floor. "You said you might come hear me sing the lead."

"I told you I'd *think* about it," Ma said, "but I've got work to do, and you know we need the money."

I didn't respond. Money was always tight, but even if she hadn't been offered that shift, Ma would've found some other excuse.

"I've got to head out," Ma said, grabbing her pass for the streetcar. "Are you sure you'll be okay walking to choir practice by yourself?"

Ma said the same thing every week. She hated it when I went anywhere alone, but I didn't have much choice since Keisha had dance class right before choir. And I wasn't about to miss rehearsal.

"I'll be fine," I said, same as every week.

Ma paused, hovering in the doorway. "It's not you I don't trust, it's . . ." She never finished that sentence, but she always relented. "Lock the door behind you when you leave. Don't talk to strangers, and follow the path I laid out for you."

I nodded, piling my empty bowl on top of the other dirty dishes in the sink. Five minutes later I was dressed in blue-jean shorts and a baggy T-shirt, ready to leave. Keisha said that being twelve meant it was time to start dressing like women instead of girls, but that was a lot easier for her since she was tall and had curves in all the right places. Me, I liked to keep things simple.

I locked the door, then hurried down the front steps, pausing for a second at the gate to glance back again. Ma said it was crazy talk, but I could swear our house was tilting. Reminded me of the houses Keisha's dad, Dwayne, built out of cards. I cocked my head to one side, willing it to stay up, then sighed and took off down the street.

Three blocks later I turned the corner and slowed a bit. My neighborhood was mostly empty—a big, boring grid of look-alike, one-story houses with no color whatsoever. The people were mostly white, the buildings were gray, and the yards were small and bare. But the area where Keisha lived was sprawling and diverse, overlapping brick apartment buildings, two-story houses painted in shades of pink, blue, and purple, with fenced-in yards, giant elephant-ear bushes, and trees with strings of Mardi Gras beads stuck in their branches.

On Keisha's street, people sat on their front steps and called their hellos to one another. Children played hopscotch and teenagers blasted music from their open car windows. I wished me and Ma could live here. How could there be such a big difference when we were only a few blocks apart?

But at least I didn't live in No-Man's-Land, where half the buildings were empty and the other half were spray-painted by gangs marking their territory. That was where police cars lingered, trash littered the streets, and no one in their right mind ventured after dark.

But the quickest way to choir practice?

Straight through the middle.

Ma would have a fit if she knew I went this way, but it would take me twice as long to walk all the way around, so I took a deep breath and forced myself forward. The key was not to stop. Keep my eyes locked ahead and my feet moving.

I hadn't gotten more than two blocks in when I saw the usual gang of men on the opposite side of the street, hanging out on the steps of a boarded-up building drinking beer. My heart raced, but I tried to look like I wasn't hurrying. I concentrated on the beat of my footsteps, and then I made up a melody and sang it in my head. I added and embellished until my focus was complete and there wasn't any part of my brain left to worry about what might be coming.

"Hey, white girl!"

A chorus of whistles and laughter shattered my song. One of the men flicked the still-glowing stub of his cigarette in my direction.

"Why don't you come over here and hang with us?" he called. It wasn't even funny, but they all laughed, slapping their knees. I walked faster, staring ahead, pretending not to smell the garbage baking in the heat or the stink of their beer. But then one of them, a young guy I didn't recognize, said something new.

"Your cracker daddy still rotting in prison?"

I looked up quick and tripped over my own feet.

How did he know about that?

No one talked about my father. Ever. Only a handful of people knew that my father was behind bars for life. Keisha and her family knew, plus my school guidance counselor, and I suspected Ms. Marion, but other than that . . .

Part of me wanted to stop and find out how this complete stranger had heard about my father, but I'm not that dumb. Instead, I scanned the horizon for the steeple of the New Heaven Baptist Church. There it was, just four blocks up, rising above the rooftops.

"Why don't you and your mama take your sorry . . ."

The guy said something real bad. Too bad to repeat. The worst thing to do is react, but I flinched, and the drunk men laughed, excited that they'd gotten a rise out of me. That's when I broke into a run. The men had won and they knew it. When I was far enough away, I glanced over my shoulder and the young guy was holding out his fingers in the shape of a gun. Aiming it at me.

A shiver raced down my spine.

Finally, I reached the church. I wiped the sweat from my forehead with one bare arm. Every muscle in my body was tense, and I wanted to retch, right there on the sidewalk.

Instead, I forced my breathing to slow down and waited for my temples to stop throbbing. I thought about the people inside: our drummers setting up, Ms. Marion organizing her papers, kids milling around, getting ready to take their places on the risers. Then I thought about the music we'd make, knowing it would wash everything away.

Soon, the outside world would be muted. The laughing men would not come in, and the music could come out. I'd open my mouth and sing so loud, I'd blow this whole rotten neighborhood away.

CHAPTER 3

FIRST THING I did once I opened the front doors of the church and stepped inside was to look for Keisha. Ms. Marion called us the Two Musketeers, which was odd since everyone knows there's supposed to be three of those, but Ms. Marion was like that, always making things out the way she wanted them to be.

"You looking for the other Musketeer?" Ms. Marion called when she saw me peering around the sanctuary.

I nodded.

"She's over near the risers."

"Thanks," I said, slipping away as quickly as I could. I found Keisha standing tall with her arms crossed, staring down Mary-Kate Torelo, one of the few other white kids in the choir. Mary-Kate was one of the girls who'd joined last month after we'd performed at the Presbyterian church uptown. There were three of them: Mary-Kate, Amber Allen, and Faith Evans. All three wore the kind of designer clothes you could only get if you were rich. They had long, spiraling hair, and they always had their nails done with decals and sparkles. Everyone knew their moms made them come, swept along by Ms. Marion's vision. But we also knew they hated every minute here.

"I'm telling you," Mary-Kate was saying, "that song wasn't even a gospel song when it was written, it was—"

Keisha cut her off. "Please," she said, "don't tell *me* about gospel."

Keisha had dark brown skin, and she usually wore her hair styled in dozens of long braids pulled back into a ponytail. She was wearing tight, curvy jeans and a fitted pink T-shirt that said DON'T MESS WITH THE PRINCESS—advice that Mary-Kate should have taken.

"You're not even African American," Keisha said, jutting out her hip. "White people don't know a thing about gospel."

Mary-Kate's eyes flashed. "That's racist," she said, even though it was obvious Keisha had only said it to bait her.

Keisha rolled her eyes. "No, it isn't," she argued. "Gospel is part of my heritage. I think I'd know if—" She stopped mid-sentence when she spotted me. "Tia! You're here!" She sprang over and wrapped her arms around me, nearly knocking me to the floor.

Mary-Kate scowled, ignoring my presence. "So if gospel is your heritage," she said to Keisha, "then why don't you have a problem with Tia singing the lead on 'I Know'?"

She meant because I was a skinny white girl with brown hair, dark brown eyes, and skin about as pale as a person's could be. Keisha didn't even pause.

"Because Tia does gospel the way it's supposed to be done," she said. "No one in the world can belt it out like she can."

Best friends are allowed to fudge the truth.

"Tia's voice is *okay,*" Mary-Kate said, "but I could sing the lead just as well. In my last choir, I was always the soloist. Everyone knows Ms. Marion plays favorites and that's why she chose Tia. Again."

At Mary-Kate's church, I'd performed a song called "A Note to God" that Ms. Marion and I had been working on during my private lessons. It wasn't usually part of our program, but Ms. Marion thought the Presbyterians would like it. Afterward, Mary-Kate's mother had sought me out to tell me how moved she'd been by my performance, while Mary-Kate had tried to murder me with her glare.

"If you hate it here so much—" Keisha started, but she never had a chance to finish because that's when Ms. Marion called us to begin rehearsal.

"C'mon, children," Ms. Marion coaxed in her thick accent. "Y'all take your places on the risers."

Ms. Marion was originally from one of the parishes outside the city—Metairie or Slidell, I could never remember which one. She didn't talk like New Orleans folk, smooth and neutral with just a hint of the south. She talked like a large, Southern woman, proud and loud.

Keisha gave Mary-Kate one last stare before pulling me onto the risers. We couldn't stand next to each other because Keisha was a soprano and I was an alto, but Keisha and I watched out for each other, so she wasn't about to leave me alone with Mary-Kate.

"Remember, children," Ms. Marion said, "you are the living, musical embodiment of Martin Luther King's dream. Make me believe it!"

As we took our places, Ms. Marion started us humming, but we were flat. We practiced in Ms. Marion's church because it was free space, but it was hot—steaming even—and the lazy ceiling fans barely made a difference. No matter how hard Ms. Marion waved us on, the Rainbow Choir swayed half a beat too slow.

Everything was heavy.

"I know y'all can do better than this," Ms. Marion chided. "Y'all can *be* better than this." Ms. Marion's voice took on the singsong cadence of a preacher. "I *know,*" she said, "don't I just know, don't I just *know,* don't I just know?" She raised one eyebrow before turning the singsong into a song-song, filling in the first words of the song we'd been practicing. "I knooooow."

She stomped one foot, shaking her arms in the air. Ms. Marion was a drama queen. In the back row the tenors started laughing and the altos covered their mouths with their hands. Ms. Marion grinned through the heat, and a bead of sweat ran down her plump cheek.

"Don't I just knoooow," she sang, stretching those words like a siren call. Off to one corner, the preacher man nodded and said "Amen, sister" as he gathered the hymn books off the red velvet pews.

"C'mon now," she said, and some of the parents clapped and whistled, cheering us on.

"Sing it, children," said old Nana Whiskers, who always came to practice even though no child belonged to her.

Ms. Marion sang, "Don't you just knooow?" turning it into a question as we hummed in the background. Then she made it a command. "Tell me if you know."

"I know," we sang in answer. Ms. Marion let our words come out loud and quick, then cut them off with a swipe of her fist.

"Do you *know*?" she asked again.

"I know," we answered.

I snuck a glance behind me. Keisha lifted her chin like she did when she was ready, Tallulah Jackson wriggled her hips, and Tyrone Sanderson stomped in rhythm to the drumbeat. Even shy Kenny Lin, the Korean tenor with the stutter, smiled in anticipation.

"One more time," Ms. Marion prodded.

"I KNOW."

Now we had it, and our words filled the small sanctuary.

"Tia," Ms. Marion said, nodding at me. I took a step forward so I was standing front and center and inhaled a deep breath. This was my moment.

I reached down inside, found the music waiting, and let it loose.

"I know that the Lord is good, that the Lord is good, that the Lord is good. That's what I know." My line soared above the choir, and I swear I felt my heart expand.

I sang like a magician pulling scarves from my sleeve. More and more scarves until it didn't seem like there could be any left. They flew up and out, every one connected to the last in a flurry of color. I sent my cool, bright sounds into the thick June air, letting the scarves weave their way through the rafters of the old church.

That's how it was that night.

The sound coming out of me was so loud, the preacher man stopped what he was doing and shut one of the big leather Bibles with a thump. Keisha's mom, Ms. Evette, sat in the first pew rocking baby Jerome back and forth. She was a large woman with close-cropped hair and beautiful high cheekbones, and her eyes were shut in appreciation. I heard her murmur *hmmm* and Jerome pointed at me with his chubby baby fingers. Old Nana Whiskers watched him and laughed like a hyena.

The sound was still coming, sucking up every scrap of breath, and behind me the choir lent their voices. They didn't sing, but they let me know they felt it too.

"All right."

"Uh-huh."

"Go Tia."

I barely heard them. They were far, far away. Right then I didn't care about anything but my song soaring through the air. I didn't care that I was a twelve-year-old girl who didn't match the size or shape of a great singer. I didn't care that my father was in prison, and me and Ma barely scraped by. I didn't care that I was at church on a Thursday evening instead of home watching TV. I didn't even care that my own mother had never once come to hear me sing.

In that moment, nothing else mattered, so I let the sound pour out.

"I knooow," I sang, pushing the volume louder and fuller than I ever had before. "I knooow," I repeated, letting the spirit take over. *"I know, I know, I know, I know."*

Everyone was clapping, hooting and hollering, lifting their hands in praise. Ms. Marion stomped her feet and the preacher man yelled, "Hallelujah!"

The sanctuary was filled with celebration. Power pulsed around me, and I sucked it inside, filling my lungs to their fullest, ready to let loose the next phrase.

Ms. Marion laughed, shaking her head and stomping her feet, and Jo Jo Lawsen held up her open palms in praise. “I believe,” she cried from the second pew. “Oh Lord, I believe.”

And in that moment, so did I.

Until the sound of gunshots shattered the air.

CHAPTER 4

ONE MINUTE I was singing loud and strong, pulling out the scarves, reaching for everything I knew was inside me, and the next moment the sound of gunfire pierced through the sanctuary. I'd heard gunshots before from far away, but these were right outside and moments later they were followed by a scream so horrible, it coursed through my body.

The sound stopped in my throat. It was a sharp stop, as if a faucet got turned off quick and hard. My chest constricted as the pastor and several of the parents who'd been watching rehearsal ran out of the building.

"Call 911!" someone yelled.

"Get the children downstairs!"

"Toil and trouble," old Nana Whiskers moaned, rocking back and forth.

Some of the sopranos started to cry as Ms. Marion and Ms. Evette herded us off the risers. "Downstairs, everyone," Ms. Marion shouted, signaling for us to go to the basement, where the adult choir stored their robes. All the kids were pressing together on the staircase, and I tried to reach Keisha, but she was too far away. My knees shook and I thought I might fall.

When we finally made it downstairs, I felt sick to my stomach and too hot in the heavy air. I was straining to find Keisha, but it was Kenny Lin who came up beside me. I didn't know Kenny very well, but he reached out and took my hand. I wanted to cling to him the way I'd clung to a float one time when I'd nearly drowned in the YMCA swimming pool. Now I felt that same blind panic, and Kenny was the only life ring around.

"It'll be o-okay," he said, working hard to get the word out despite his stutter. He held my hand for a long time, and I was surprised he didn't let go. His hand felt warm and smooth, and every time I started to tense up, he squeezed lightly as if to remind me he was there. No other boy would've done that, and I wasn't sure if I should thank him or try to pretend it was no big deal, but before I'd decided, there were footsteps on the stairs.

"Police are here," one of the parents hollered. "They said we can bring 'em back upstairs."

That should have been a relief, except now there was even more chaos as everyone tried to get up the stairs we'd just come down. In the crush, Kenny's hand dropped away from mine and we were pushed apart. When we reached the top, all the parents who'd been watching rehearsal were waiting and they scooped up their children right away, hugging them tight.

I couldn't help wishing someone was there for me.

"Don't leave the building," Ms. Marion yelled. "Everyone stay inside until the police say it's safe to go out."

I looked around for Kenny and saw his rumpled figure beside Mark Whitmore. My face flushed when he caught my eye. I'd never held hands with a boy before. *Why had he helped me?*

Everyone was asking about what happened, and finally the pastor came back in from outside, and the look on his face was so full of horror, I knew that someone must have died. There was blood on his right hand, a thin streak from the thumb to the wrist, and I couldn't stop staring at it. He wiped it off right away, but the image was branded in my brain.

"The devil is roaming," he breathed. "Oh Lord . . ."

He mumbled a prayer as Ms. Marion hurried down the aisle with the other adults. They met him by the door, talking in hushed voices, and I saw Ms. Marion's hand fly to her mouth. I strained to hear what they were saying, but it was impossible over the sirens.

Eventually, Ms. Marion came back, frowning and pushing us toward the risers.

"Come on, children," she said, "we're going to sing the darkness out. No use standing around here letting evil devour us. Might as well keep busy until the police say it's okay to leave."

"What happened?" Keisha asked, her voice rising above the babble.

"Nothing y'all need to worry about," Ms. Marion said. "You're safe, and that's the important thing."

"Did someone get hurt?" Mary-Kate demanded.

Ms. Marion nodded. "Yes, but they've been transported to the hospital and they'll be given the best possible care."

"I want to go home," Amanda Chen said, starting to cry again.

"Now, now," Ms. Marion chided. "Let's focus on something else. Your parents will take you home very soon, but until then you're all safe. I promise."

That was a lie. Around here, safe was a wish, not a promise.

"Come on. Places, children. Take deep, supported breaths. Everyone breathe together now."

We trickled back onto the risers, and Ms. Marion tapped one finger against her music stand. "Let's pick up where we left off. From the top."

It didn't seem right to pretend as if nothing was wrong, but I could hear my mother's voice: *Like it or not, life goes on, Tia Rose.*

"Tia," Ms. Marion said, nodding for me to step forward.

I relaxed my jaw, trying to remember the way I'd felt

before everything shattered, but my face was flushed and blotchy. I pictured the blood on the pastor's hand, and my stomach flipped like an undercooked pancake.

"Let's try to add more soul this time," Ms. Marion was saying. She was stalling, trying to settle us down, so I breathed deep. The bass section squeaked out a *hmmm,* but the choir didn't sway. Sweat trickled down my forehead, and the world began to tilt.

No matter how hard I tried, I couldn't fill my lungs.

Ms. Marion leaned forward. "Tia? You okay?"

I meant to say yes, but I fainted instead.

CHAPTER 5

THE SOUND of whispering tickled my ears. It seemed to be coming from far away, and no matter how hard I tried, I couldn't make out whole sentences, but I caught certain words. Important ones.

Tia's father...

...life without parole...

...horrible memories...

I recognized the voices: Ms. Evette, Ms. Marion, and Mary-Kate's mother. Why were they talking about my father?

Seemed strange. I was only four when he went to jail, so I had no memories of him: not the sound or smell or look of him. We didn't visit or write, and no parole meant he'd never come home again, which, according to Ma, was a good thing.

He's dead to us, Tia Rose. When your father committed

that robbery, he walked away from this family forever. Don't let me catch you wasting your time, dwelling on that man.

But now, all these years later, people were talking as if my father had reached out from the Louisiana State Penitentiary to push me off the risers.

Didn't make any sense.

I opened my eyes, squinting a bit, and saw wooden giraffes hovering over my face—Ms. Evette's big old dangling earrings.

"Tia," she said, stroking my hair. "Thank goodness you're awake."

I lifted my head, and Ms. Evette breathed out a long, loud sigh of relief. "That's right. Lift it up to the Lord," she said, as if I were praying instead of lying in a heap.

Beside her, Mary-Kate's mom waved a fan over me, and I could see her daughter scowling from the risers. Kenny was making his way to the front row, his face creased with worry, and I wondered why he seemed to care so much.

Something hot and sticky trickled down my cheek and without thinking, I reached up to wipe it away, only now there was blood on my hand and that nearly made me faint again. I've always hated the sight of blood. Even a drop can make my vision narrow to black and my breath catch until I think I might suffocate.

Ms. Marion turned. "Someone get a wet paper towel for Tia's cut."

Kenny bolted off the risers, and I tried hard to keep my bearings.

"That was quite a spill you took," Ms. Marion said, bustling me into a sitting position. "I'm so sorry. I never should have pushed you to sing. I thought it would help, but—"

"I'm okay," I lied.

Ms. Marion frowned. "We should take you to the emergency room."

I shook my head. Emergency room visits cost money Ma and I didn't have. "I'm fine," I said, clearing my throat. "I should've told you I wasn't ready, that's all."

Right then Kenny came back with a wet wad of paper towels. "H-here," he said, and his eyes were so worried, I had to look away.

"I'm a nurse," Mary-Kate's mom told me. "I can check for a concussion."

Old Nana Whiskers launched into a stream of gibberish. "Went to the hospital and never came out! Those doctors just ate her up! Guns, sirens, and hospitals gonna eat Tia up."

I felt all the kids in choir gaping at me, and my cheeks burned in humiliation. Amber Allen and Faith Evans were snickering, whispering behind their hands. I gave Keisha a look that begged her to save me, but she just shrugged helplessly as Mary-Kate's mom shined a penlight in my eyes and asked me tons of questions. Finally, she nodded.

"You look okay, sweetie," she said, pushing her blond hair behind her ears, "but you'll want to get checked out just in case. Have your mother drive you to a clinic once you get home, all right?"

I managed a fake smile. "I will," I said. "I'm sure I just got overheated from running up and down the stairs."

Ms. Marion and Ms. Evette exchanged glances, and there was something hidden in the corner of their eyes. None of it made sense, but I suddenly felt cold even though the sanctuary had to be a hundred degrees. I hugged my arms tight around my body.

"I'm fine," I whispered again even though this time no one had asked.

Ms. Marion pinched the bridge of her nose the way she did when she was upset. More parents were starting to arrive, bursting in full of panic, and the pastor was calming them, but I knew Ms. Marion wanted to be there too.

"Go ahead," I told her.

Ms. Evette nodded toward the doors. "Go. I'll stay with Tia."

Ms. Marion paused, wiping the sweat from her brow, but then she sighed and made her way up front. A police officer stepped inside the church and I could see the relief on everyone's faces when he said we could go home.

"Okay, children," Ms. Marion shouted over the noise. "If your guardians are here, you may leave. I'll wait with anyone who needs to stay. If June Fest is canceled I'll activate our phone tree, otherwise I'll see you all tomorrow night. This community will need your voices now more than ever, so be prepared to sing!"

Keisha jumped down from the risers and took her baby brother, Jerome, from Mrs. Chen, who'd been holding him while Ms. Evette took care of me. Jerome tugged at her braids. "Let's get out of here," Keisha said. "This was the worst night ever."

My heart panged. Was it horrible to feel disappointed about choir being cut short? Someone had just gotten shot, maybe even killed, and I was unhappy to lose an hour of rehearsal? But I couldn't help the surge of sadness.

"What do you think happened?" I asked Keisha, brushing myself off as I stood. "Do you think . . ." I couldn't bring myself to say it. "I mean, do you think it was . . ."

"A robbery gone bad? Like your dad?" Keisha shook her head. "No. I'm sure that wasn't it. I bet you anything this was gang related. You know those fools are always shooting at each other. Serves them right if one of 'em gets hit."

I wanted to believe that was true. I even thought about those men who'd taunted me on my way to rehearsal, but something about the pastor's face and the woman's scream made me sure this hadn't been the kind of violence anyone could shrug off.

"Let's go," Keisha said. "This place is giving me the creeps."

I followed her to the door, but before I could slip away, Kenny caught up to me.

"Are you sure you're o-o—"

Bruce Abrams banged into him from behind. "Move it, l-l-loser."

There was a crowd of boys heading for the door and all of them snickered while Kenny blushed.

"Don't listen to them," I said. "You'd think they'd get tired of the same old jokes."

Kenny nodded, but he still didn't look up. "Can I get you a drink of w-water or something? You look f-f-f—"

It was wrong to rush him, but I couldn't help it. When Kenny stuttered, it was hard not to get impatient. "Flushed?"

Kenny sighed. "Yeah."

I shook my head. "No thanks. I have to go."

Kenny glanced at the doorway as his mother burst in, fear etched on her face. I could tell he wanted to say something else, but he didn't try.

"Well . . . g-g-g-good night," he said instead.

I studied his dark tousled hair and his deep, coffee-brown eyes. Kenny was kind of handsome when you stopped to look at him. "Good night," I said, wishing he'd said whatever it was he'd been thinking.

"Ready?" Keisha called, waiting by the door.

"Yeah."

I glanced around the sanctuary one more time. Kids and parents were pairing off, bustling around as they gathered up their things. Was I the only one who still heard the gunshots?

I touched my head where I'd cut myself, expecting to see blood on my fingers, but there was nothing.

Nothing to show that everything had changed.

CHAPTER 6

POLICE CARS filled the road outside the church, their red and blue lights flashing silently under the neon-pink sunset. Made my nerves prickle. I knew Ms. Evette and Keisha felt it too, because Keisha was stone-cold quiet, and usually she never stopped jabbering. She'd handed Jerome back to her ma, and now Ms. Evette hugged him tight to her chest.

In the middle of the police was a single car with a bullet hole through the back window. Spiderwebbed cracks extended outward on the glass. Yellow caution tape marked off the area around the car where three officers stood writing in little white notepads. They looked up when they saw us, and their eyes stopped on me. They looked at Ms. Evette like she was stealing me. I knew that Ms. Marion wanted us to believe in a rainbow vision, but I suspected these cops still saw things in black and white.

Ms. Evette raised her chin defiantly, as if daring them to say anything.

"Move along," one of the officers grumbled. Baby Jerome pointed at the policeman and Ms. Evette pressed his soft belly against her waist. I paused, studying the bullet hole, and Keisha gave me a look that said *hurry up.* I meant to follow, but I couldn't stop staring.

It was odd the way the car sat there in the road. Not parked near the sidewalk, but abandoned as if the driver had run out of gas. It was old, and I knew I'd seen it before. That made my heart beat faster and my stomach churn. Ms. Evette held out her hand. It was time to move on, but I kept looking back, wondering *Who? What? Why?*

I stumbled the rest of the way home, my feet betraying me on every step.

When we finally reached my house, Ms. Evette peered in through the front window. "Your mother is home, right?"

I felt like a worn-out quilt, unraveling. "Of course," I mumbled, although it wasn't true.

Ms. Evette sighed. "I hate leaving you when there's just been a shooting and you've had a fall. I'd rather talk to your mother first."

"She's sleeping," I said. "But don't worry. I'll wake Ma up as soon as I get in."

"Tia," Keisha said, "why don't you run inside and ask your mama if you can sleep over tonight? If she's asleep, why would you want to—"

I put my key in the lock and thrust the door open.

"I can't," I said. "Not tonight."

Ms. Evette's frown deepened. "You're *certain* your mother is inside? Asleep?"

"Of course," I said. "Why would I lie about that?"

"Well . . ." Ms. Evette said, and I knew she couldn't figure out the answer to that question. "All right. It's getting late and I need to get Jerome home to bed. Tia, you lock this door the second you get inside, and you wake that mother of yours up immediately. Do you hear me? Tell her everything. Understand?"

I nodded. "Yes, ma'am," I said, stepping inside my dark, empty house. I shut the door behind me and doubled-locked it, leaving the chain off for Ma to come in later.

Then I slid down the back of the door and closed my eyes.

What had happened tonight? Something awful. But why hadn't the adults told us what it was? Was it so horrible they thought we shouldn't know? Maybe that was okay for the nine- and ten-year-olds, but most of us were older now. We even had a few fourteen-year-old guys in the bass section.

A flash of anger surged through me, and for just a moment I hated those adults for keeping secrets—Ms. Marion, Ms. Evette, Mary-Kate's mom, the pastor—but then I tamped the feeling down because none of this was their fault.

They didn't shoot anyone.

But someone had.

CHAPTER 7

THE NEXT MORNING, I woke with my sheets twisted around my ankles and my forehead drenched with sweat. I'd had nightmares, tossing and turning all night, waking to the sound of imaginary gunshots, only to fall asleep again and dream about Ma driving the car with the bullet hole in the back window and my father standing in the road with his fingers shaped into a gun. In the dream I screamed until I was hoarse.

It was a relief to finally see daylight, but the feeling was short-lived. I'd never dreamed about my father before. Not that I could remember. It'd been a long time since I'd last asked Ma about him. I'd been six, maybe seven? Old enough to wonder if Daddy was ever coming home, but not old enough to understand the answer. I shivered, remembering the coldness in Ma's eyes, as if she'd been angry at me for asking.

I'll answer your questions this once, but after this you

need to understand: Your father is dead to us, and there's nothing new to say about a dead man.

I tried to remember my mother's exact words about what he'd done, but the facts were scattered in my brain—just out of reach. I wanted to force them to the surface, but I was exhausted. My stomach churned, creating a sour taste in my mouth, and I swallowed hard before stumbling into the bathroom and splashing cold water onto my face. I didn't even bother to warm up my vocal cords. For the first time I could remember, I didn't want to sing.

When I finally made it to the kitchen, I was surprised to see Ma still up, sitting at the worn table we used for meals. Ma rarely stayed up after she worked a night shift, and she looked tired. She also looked hard as iron.

"There was a shooting last night," she said, without even saying good morning. "Near your church."

It wasn't a question, but I nodded. "How did you hear?"

"Morning edition got delivered to the store just before I left."

She pushed a newspaper across the table. The front page had a black-and-white photo of the abandoned car, and a fragment of the church was visible in the background. The headline screamed, INFANT KILLED, GUNMEN FLED.

I gave an involuntary gasp. *"A baby."*

Immediately, I thought of Keisha's brother, Jerome. He was eleven months old now, all big brown eyes and rolls of fat.

I sat down heavy, my legs giving way beneath me. Ma hesitated, like she wasn't sure what to do. Finally, she reached over and patted my hand before drawing back to scrape at a splotch of dried ketchup on the table with her fingernail. Then she stood abruptly and went over to the refrigerator to get out the eggs. Her movements were quick and jerky, as if she couldn't decide whether to comfort me or punish me.

"So, did this happen during your rehearsal?" she asked. "Why didn't you call me at work?"

I mumbled something about not wanting to bother her, and Ma grunted a response, but what that response meant, I couldn't be sure. She moved to the stove and scrambled the eggs while I read the newspaper article.

The baby, ten months old, had been shot by accident during an attempted carjacking. Two gunmen had fled on foot and police were trying to locate them. There was a number to call if anyone had information, and there was also a picture of the baby and his mother.

"The Raven woman," I breathed. It was the dark-haired woman who lived on Seventh Street. She didn't speak English and dressed in long skirts and shirts with flowing sleeves. We didn't really know where she was from, but Keisha and I thought she looked like a raven because her hair was so black it almost shone blue. Plus there was something mystical about her that made it seem as if she might take flight. She lived with her husband and her—

No, not her son. Not anymore.

For a split second, the world went fuzzy, like it had before I fainted. But this time I held on, forcing my fists to unclench and my breathing to slow.

"Tia?" Ma studied me hard and then she walked over to snatch the paper off the table. Ma's auburn hair was pulled into a sloppy ponytail, tied back with an old gray scrunchie. The lines on her face were strained as she dished me my scrambled eggs and cheddar grits. "You aren't dwelling, are you?"

Dwelling was what Ma called it when I thought too much about bad stuff. I didn't answer, and she frowned.

"Now look," she said, real stern, as if dwelling were something I could get grounded for doing. "What happened to that baby is horrible, and we will hope for justice and mercy, but this burden isn't yours to carry. We've each of us got our own burdens and they're plenty big enough. Do you understand?"

She looked me in the eyes and I nodded, but I'd already thought about those gunshots again. *Why do things like this happen?*

A voice whispered in response.

Because of people like your father.

I pushed the food around on my plate until I couldn't sit still any longer. Then I stood up. "I'm going to meet Keisha early and hang out at her house today," I said, trying to make my voice sound normal. "The choir's singing at the festival tonight, so Ms. Evette will bring me home."

Ma said, "Finish your breakfast," and gave me a good hard stare until I sat back down and shoved in another bite of eggs and two more bites of grits. They tasted like paste and I could hardly make my throat swallow.

"I'm not sure I like the idea of your choir being out so soon after—"

"I'm *not* skipping choir," I said. "I sing the lead, so I have to be there."

Ma took a step back, and I could tell she was surprised that I could be hard as iron too.

I softened. "You could come tonight. Hear me sing."

Ma was shaking her head before the words were even out. "I've got auctioning to do online."

I looked at her as she stooped to pick up a giant stuffed dog from the kitchen floor. "Ms. Evette will be at June Fest," I said. "She works a side job too."

I couldn't believe I'd said that, but Ma pretended she didn't hear. "I've got to get this boxed and into the mail," she said, shuffling toward her bedroom, where she kept the postal scale.

I opened my mouth, then closed it again, scraping my fork against my plate. It made a sound like nails on a chalkboard, which I knew drove Ma crazy. So I did it again. Finally, Ma snapped.

"Fine. Go to Keisha's then. Lock the door when you leave. Don't talk to strangers, and call me if you have any problems."

Same thing she said every day.

"Fine," I echoed, getting up to leave. "I'll stay out of trouble."

But even as I said those words, I knew they were a lie. Trouble was like a hurricane. If you were in its path, it would barrel down on top of you, no matter how hard you tried to shore things up.

CHAPTER 8

I BOLTED OUT the door, taking off toward Keisha's apartment. Usually I sang while I walked, marking time with my feet, but that day I couldn't sing a note. My whole body felt hot and tense, coiled like a rusty spring. When you sing, your body has to open up: lungs, diaphragm, throat, shoulders. Even parts that don't seem involved with making music need to let loose, like when you lift your chin and straighten your back.

Imagine the top of your head lifting off, letting your spirit free, and then the music overflows.

I could hear Ms. Marion's voice, but I couldn't unclench my muscles. By the time I got to Keisha's, I still hadn't found that place in me where my singing should have been.

I took the outside emergency staircase one flight up to Keisha's floor. The metal frame was already hot from the sun, so I puffed on my fingers after I pried the window open. Keisha must have heard me coming, because she appeared and reached out to pull me inside.

"You're here early," she said. She was still in her pajamas, her braids loose and disheveled, looking crazy with flyaway curls. She chewed on her lower lip, and there was something odd about the way she looked at me, as if she wished I'd arrived later. Or maybe hadn't come at all? But that was silly. I practically lived at Keisha's house.

I waited for her to start our secret handshake.

"Well?" I said at last.

"Oh." Keisha let out her breath in a nervous whoosh and held out her hands.

Shimmer, shimmer,

superstars,

Keisha and Tia,

we'll go far.

We smacked our hands together, up and down, side, side, then once in the middle. It barely rhymed, but we'd only been in second grade when we'd made it up.

"Tia? That you?" Ms. Evette called.

"Yes ma'am. Ma says hey," I lied.

Ms. Evette sashayed into the doorway. "You feeling better today? How's that cut?"

"It's healing," I said, flopping down on Keisha's purple comforter.

Ms. Evette glanced at Keisha, then cocked her head to one side. "Did you see the paper this morning?" she asked me.

I nodded.

"And did you talk to your mother about what happened?"

I hesitated only a moment before nodding again. Technically, it wasn't a lie.

"There's going to be a vigil for the baby at June Fest tonight," Ms. Evette said. "I spoke to Marion this morning and she'd like the choir to perform the song you've been practicing, if you feel up to singing the lead. Is your ma coming out?"

I shook my head, but I noticed the way Ms. Evette hadn't really waited for an answer. In fact, she almost seemed relieved, which was strange because normally she got exasperated real quick when it came to Ma not showing up for things.

"Well, you girls keep it down in here."

As soon as Ms. Evette stepped away, Keisha queued up "Pyramid" on her laptop. It was an old pop song by Charice that had been our favorite when we were nine years old—the one that convinced us to join the Rainbow Choir. Keisha hadn't played it in a long time, though, and I'd started to think we might be outgrowing it. I wondered why she'd chosen that song today.

Keisha drummed her fingers in rhythm, and her eyes danced around the room, landing anywhere other than my face. "I'm surprised your ma didn't lock you in the house today," she said at last.

I snorted. "Me too."

Keisha opened her mouth, and then she shut it again, as if she'd changed her mind about what she'd been meaning to say. When "Pyramid" ended, Keisha didn't queue up anything else, and we were quiet for a long time.

"Were you scared last night?" Keisha asked at last. "I thought someone was going to bust into the church and we'd all end up on the news, like one of those school shootings. Me and Ma stayed up late talking about it."

Even now I could hear the *pop, pop, pop* of the gunshots. I'd been terrified.

"Kenny Lin held my hand," I said. "I was looking for you, and I guess I must have seemed scared, because he came up beside me and said everything would be okay."

"C-c-crazy Kenny did that?" Keisha said, her eyebrows shooting up. "Wow. I never would've guessed he had it in him. He's so quiet."

"I know," I said. "But it was nice. I mean—"

I hadn't even finished my sentence before Keisha was tossing one of her pillows at me. "Do you *like* him? Do *not* tell me you have a crush on Kenny Lin."

My cheeks burned. "I never said that."

"You didn't have to," Keisha said, flopping backward. "I can see it on your face."

Instead of responding, I crossed my eyes, and that made Keisha laugh. It was impossible to win an argument with her, so it was better not to start up in the first place. For a moment, things felt normal between us, but just as quickly, the feeling slipped away.

"So did you really talk to your mother about the shooting?" Keisha asked.

I shrugged. "Sort of. Ma told me not to dwell on it."

"Figures."

My brows creased. "What's that supposed to mean?"

Keisha got that look in her eyes—the one she got when she wasn't messing around. "It means your mother doesn't like it when you think about bad things because she doesn't want you to ask any questions. She wants you to live in a bubble."

I paused. "Well, it's not like we can change any of the bad stuff that happens, so what's the use in knowing about it?"

It's useless to live in the past, Tia Rose. Keep your eyes ahead, never behind.

Keisha got real quiet. "If it were me . . . I'd rather know the truth."

There was something Keisha wasn't telling me. A cold prickle ran up the length of my body. "Why are you acting so strange?"

Keisha poked her finger into the split seam of her purple beanbag chair. "Tia," she said at last, "if I knew something about your father . . . something my mom told me last night . . . would you want to know? I mean, if it was bad news, would you still want me to tell you?"

I drew in my breath.

There's nothing new to say about a dead man.

Of course I should say yes. But once I knew, there would

be no taking it back. Ever. I felt like a little kid, wishing I could cover my ears tight and sing nonsense syllables at the top of my lungs.

"Say it," I said, at last. "Quick, before I chicken out."

Keisha nodded, as if she understood. She took a deep breath. "Your father isn't in prison for armed robbery," she said. "He's in prison for . . ."

Murder.

". . . murder."

I'd thought the word even before Keisha said it, but how could I know that? It wasn't even true. I shook my head. "No . . . that isn't . . . Ma told me what happened . . ."

The facts came back like puzzle pieces before you put them together.

1) My father had gotten drunk and robbed someone.
2) He'd had a gun and used it.
3) He hid from the police and fought them after his arrest.
4) There had been a trial.
5) This wasn't my father's first arrest. He'd had a series of smaller arrests that made the judge decide he'd run out of chances.
6) Ma had decided the same thing.
7) I'd never been given a choice.

I didn't say any of that out loud.

Keisha studied her feet. "Well, if she didn't tell you that he killed someone, then she didn't tell you the whole story. Ma said it was a big deal around here and that's why your mom hates to go out in public."

I could feel tears pricking the back of my eyelids. My father had killed someone? That couldn't be true. But even as part of my brain denied the idea, another part knew this was real.

Who else knew? Ms. Evette? Ms. Marion? People in the neighborhood? Everyone besides me?

"No," I said, trying to force the truth back into hiding. "Ma wouldn't lie to me about something this important. And besides, I'd know. Sure, I was a little kid, but I was still there!"

Keisha shrugged. "You told me you don't remember your father, so maybe that includes . . . what he did."

"What did your mother tell you?" I said, forcing the words out of my mouth. "Who did he kill?"

Keisha shook her head. "She wouldn't say. Ma thinks you already know, and she said if you weren't telling, then I'd have to wait until you were ready. But I was sure you wouldn't have hid something this big. Not from me."

I shook my head. "I know my father robbed someone, and Ma said he was armed, but . . ."

Ma didn't always tell the truth.

Keisha paused. "You know, there's a way we could find out exactly what your father did, if you really want to know."

Her gaze slid to her computer.

The idea made my blood run cold, but I always told myself not to be a coward. Like walking through No-Man's-Land: Keep moving forward, no matter what.

Could I do that now?

"Okay," I said at last.

"Here goes," Keisha said. She typed in *Lyle Frank, murder, New Orleans, robbery.* I couldn't help wondering what kind of list I'd have behind my name when I got older.

We both held our breath.

Whatever happened had been horrible enough to make Ma ashamed, even in our own home. Had he killed someone she'd known? A priest or nun? What if he'd killed a police officer?

But even with all of those horrible thoughts running through my brain, I didn't expect the last piece of the puzzle until it clicked into place.

Lyle Frank Charged with Murder of Girl, 12.

Blood rushed to my toes, my ears thrumming with the dull roar I'd heard right before I fainted. Keisha made a strangled noise, and then she angled the laptop away, but I reached out and turned the computer screen back toward me.

Child Dead After Fatal Robbery.

Family Mourns Loss of Beloved Daughter.

Lyle Frank Convicted of Murder, Sentenced to Life.

The list of links went on and on. I clicked one, forcing

air in and out of my lungs, and then she was there looking back at me: the girl my father had killed.

Danielle Morton.

She looked a lot like Keisha. She had deep brown skin, sparkling dark brown eyes, and she wore her hair pulled back in a ponytail. Her T-shirt had a treble clef on it, with butterflies taking the place of the notes on a scale.

"No," I whispered. "No, no, no."

My fingers reached out to touch the screen.

I clicked on another link and then another, and they were like pieces to a whole new puzzle, falling into place.

1) My father's mug shot.
2) A photo of Danielle's family leaving the church after her funeral.
3) An article about Danielle's school releasing pink balloons in her memory.
4) A grainy picture of my mother leaving the courthouse after my father's sentencing.
5) My father in an orange jumpsuit, being led out of the courtroom, his hands cuffed behind his back.

The whole story was laid out in a hundred different versions, but all the facts remained the same. My father had been out drinking. He'd broken into the Mortons' house late at night, shot their only daughter during the course of a robbery, narrowly escaped through a back window, and then hid from police before being caught.

And as a footnote?

Lyle Frank is the father of a four-year-old girl.

Eight years ago, I'd been a footnote in an article about murder.

I slammed the laptop shut.

"Are you okay?" Keisha asked.

I shook my head.

My temples throbbed, and I opened Keisha's window to get some air, but all I could do was look out over the streets of New Orleans, knowing that somewhere, a family had been destroyed because of what my father had done.

"Keisha," I whispered, "I have to get out of here."

All morning I'd wanted to get to Keisha's place, but now all I wanted to do was leave.

"I'll go with you," Keisha said, her face a mask of worry.

I shook my head. "Please. I need to be alone. I just have to . . . get out." Silence hung in the room, but Keisha has my back, even when she doesn't like it.

"Okay," she said at last, "but don't you dare do anything stupid, and if you let anything happen to you, I'll be so sore, you won't ever hear the end of it."

I could only nod.

Keisha watched me escape out the window, and I saw the worry in her eyes. I felt bad, but not bad enough to stay. I climbed down the fire escape, ducking under the overhanging limbs of the magnolia tree.

If Keisha had asked, I couldn't have said where I was going, but somewhere deep inside, I'd already made up my mind. I was drawn by a powerful force, like the Mississippi River flowing relentlessly into the sea.

CHAPTER 9

My father had killed *a girl.*

The sun was high in the sky now, and it beat down on me as I ran, sweat soaking my neck, trickling along my spine. I sprinted past my block, but kept on going. A few open windows let out the sounds of babies crying and mothers hollering. Dogs barked in the distance.

I needed to find that baby's mama.

When school was in session, Keisha and I had walked past the baby's house every day. Sometimes there was music escaping from within—songs with syncopated beats and tinsely chimes. There were often people coming and going, and not a single one of them seemed to speak English, so we didn't know where they were really from or how they'd ended up in New Orleans. Ma said maybe they were Ukranian, but I'd heard Ms. Evette say she thought they might be from Poland.

Now people were gathered in the yard, all dressed in

black. It had never occurred to me that anyone else would be there, and I felt stupid for not guessing as much. Just because me and Ma didn't have any friends or family didn't mean other people didn't have them.

I hid behind the wide trunk of an oak tree, panting from my hard run, watching the people come and go. The front door was wide open and guests lingered on the steps and around the iron gate. Their lilting voices were hushed, saying words I couldn't understand. Some of the women wore dark veils, and the men had solemn faces. What would they think if they knew I was hiding there, watching them?

In front of the house was a makeshift shrine with candles, teddy bears, cards, and flowers, and it made me ashamed that I hadn't brought anything. There was only one thing I had to give that anyone would care about, and I pictured myself standing there, singing something beautiful next to that wall of sadness—singing "A Note to God," the same song I'd sung at the Presbyterian church.

Grant us the faith to carry on

Give us hope when it seems all hope is gone

I'd watched videos of Charice performing this song, and I'd tried to capture the way she closed her eyes and drew out each note until it was so deep and full, it overflowed. Usually, I could do the same, but now I wondered if these people would want anything I had to offer.

I thought about what Ms. Marion always told me: *It*

takes beauty to make beauty. Love yourself and your voice will be a gift to others.

But Ms. Marion had no idea how messed-up my life was. Who could love that?

Outside, people moved to and from the memorial fence with quiet ease, laying down their small offerings before turning away, while my heart ached. I knew it was time to go back to Keisha's apartment before she got too worried and told her mother I'd gone. Whatever answers I thought I'd find here were swallowed up by a single thought: I shouldn't have come.

Turning, I stepped away from my hiding spot behind the oak tree. From somewhere inside, a strong smell was wafting out through the open windows, unfamiliar spices drenching my senses. I wrapped my arms around myself and breathed in deep, tasting something tangy on my tongue. Then I reached out with one hand to steady myself against the rough, gnarled bark of the tree trunk. I felt eyes on me, and glanced up.

That's when I saw her.

At the window on the second floor was the Raven woman. She wore a tattered black shawl and her dark, flowing hair spilled around her shoulders. Her face looked as gray as the worn sidewalk, and her eyes said things about grief I couldn't bear to think about. Made me suck in my breath, fast and hard.

Her gaze rested on me. Did she know who I was? Or did

she see a little kid, too shy to come forward and honor her son?

She pressed one palm against the glass.

Every inch of me wanted to run, but I stared back. The only thing I could do was to hold her gaze without allowing myself to flinch.

CHAPTER 10

WHEN I GOT back to Keisha's place, I napped fitfully, curled up on the couch with the sound of the outdoors drifting in through the open window. I imagined I was Danielle Morton—still alive—and tried to see my life through her eyes. I listened to the cars and trucks passing on the street and the clang of people's steps on the fire escape. I heard old Nana Whiskers calling for her cat, and Tyrone Rathbone yelling at Werner Mayfield, who always parked in front of the fire hydrant. I smelled the garbage truck as the men loaded the rubbish, and I could almost taste the odor on my tongue. I shut my eyes tight and let every detail of the day wash over me, painful and brilliant all at once.

At five o'clock, Ms. Evette came in and sat down beside me. She put one cool hand on my forehead. "Do you think you're up to singing at June Fest? Maybe you should stay here instead. I'd be happy to keep you company."

Keisha was sitting at the opposite end of the couch, and

I knew what she was thinking. That afternoon, Khalil from choir had texted her, wanting to meet up after our performance. Keisha had never made plans with a boy before, not like this, and best friends didn't miss that kind of thing. What if something went wrong and she needed me? And if things went right, who would she tell?

I forced a smile. "I'm just tired," I lied. "I didn't sleep well last night. I'll take a shower and get ready to go."

Ms. Evette hesitated, but I got up and headed to the bathroom without waiting for her answer.

Keisha caught my arm as I went by. "I'm glad you're coming tonight," she said. "I know you're upset about your dad, but I'd bet you anything we're the only ones who know. Nothing's changed. You'll see."

I nodded. "Yeah. I'm sure you're right."

But as much as I wanted the truth about my father to disappear like water circling down the drain, I already understood that wouldn't happen.

Like it or not, life goes on, Tia Rose.

That's what Ma always said. But even that was a lie.

For some people . . . it didn't.

~

By the time we left for June Fest, the stifling heat had died down a bit and there wasn't a cloud in sight. Jerome was laughing his bubbly baby laugh, and Keisha was playing peek-a-boo with him behind her mother's back. Her dad, Dwayne, whistled as we walked.

Ms. Evette and Dwayne had met in high school, and the way Dwayne told it, he'd been the biggest geek in the whole of New Orleans, with thick glasses and buckteeth. Dwayne said he'd had a crush on Ms. Evette even in high school, but he couldn't get up the courage to ask her out until he'd grown into his teeth. Now he had huge muscles and a shaved head, and no one would ever think he'd been a scrawny kid with acne.

Watching the two of them walking hand in hand made me think things might not be so bad, but as soon as we arrived at the festival, I felt the tension in the air.

June Fest was an annual community gathering held outdoors, in the courtyard beside the old Catholic church. The Catholics didn't organize the event, but they lent out their courtyard since it was a nice, safe place. The area was large, and there was an ivy-covered wall surrounding the yard, so you could relax instead of always looking over your shoulder.

Every year there was a different theme. Last year was a carnival theme, and this year's theme was supposed to be literacy, but it had obviously been changed at the last minute. The courtyard walls were decorated with baby-blue ribbons, and a huge banner proclaimed, SUPPORT VICTIMS OF VIOLENCE. Giant posters were emblazoned with the same photo of the baby that had been in the newspaper, and someone had set up a wall with hundreds of photographs on it, all of them victims of violent crime. My heart thrummed with nervous tension. Somewhere on that wall I'd find Danielle's picture.

I stopped, sucking in a deep breath, and glanced at Keisha, but she was studying the crowd, probably looking for Khalil. I wished I'd stayed behind like Ms. Evette had said, but it was too late to change my mind now.

Dwayne carried a long card table for Ms. Evette's jewelry, and me and Keisha carried the boxes with her mother's hand-carved creations. Ms. Evette found a spot in the front and put out her sign—EVETTE'S TREASURES—and then she set about arranging each necklace and earring real artistically. The whole time Dwayne stood behind her, laughing and moving stuff out of place so she'd swat at him. Dwayne will do just about anything to make someone laugh.

On one side of Ms. Evette, Lyle Pots was selling stationery and on the other side, old Mrs. White had embroidered pillows for sale. They both greeted Ms. Evette, Dwayne, and even Keisha, but when it came to me, their eyes slipped away.

"C'mon," Keisha said, oblivious. "Let's check things out."

I followed, trying not to imagine people staring.

Keisha and I moved past the risers where we'd perform and the podium where community leaders would make their speeches. The New Heaven Baptist Church had a bake sale booth, and the YMCA's literacy program was painting faces for the little kids. There were animal balloons and hair braiding, and someone had rented an old-fashioned popcorn machine. It should have been fun, but it wasn't.

"That's the kid whose father shot that poor girl."

"I'm surprised she showed up tonight."

The hair on my neck stood on end. All around me I caught slips of conversation I wasn't meant to overhear, and I could tell Keisha heard them too. She pulled me along the way she usually dragged Jerome, so fast he had to toddle on his tiptoes.

We made our way over to a booth near the back of the courtyard, where a woman I didn't recognize was setting out handmade soaps. I grabbed one and held it to my nose, inhaling its floral scent. Felt good to smell something nice, and my shoulders relaxed a bit. I wondered if this was what aromatherapy meant. Me and Keisha had read about that once in a magazine. The headline had said *10 Ways to Pamper Yourself* but all the ideas had cost money, like getting your nails done or going to the movies.

"Try this one," Keisha said, handing me a white soap labeled PEPPERMINT. I could tell she was trying to distract me, and I wanted it to work. We sniffed lavender, sea mist, green tea, patchouli, coconut, lemon-lime, and vanilla. Finally, I picked up a cucumber-scented soap, feeling the smooth weight of it against my palm, but the woman in charge of the booth snatched it away.

"That's enough," she snapped.

Keisha and I both looked up, our jaws falling open.

"Go on," the woman said. "If you're not buying, move along."

She was staring straight at me. I turned and walked away, willing myself not to cry. For a moment, Keisha just stood there, and I thought she was going to argue, but then she followed me instead.

"What a nasty woman," she said when she'd caught up to me.

"We should find Ms. Marion," I muttered.

We walked slower this time, neither of us saying a word. The barbecue grills were heating up, sending waves of stomach-rumbling smoke in our direction. Old Mr. Hill was stirring a big pot of jambalaya, and the Neighborhood Association was making po' boys. I'd hardly eaten breakfast or lunch, so my stomach was clamoring, but I couldn't imagine eating anything now. Keisha followed my gaze, wistfully.

"Better wait until after we sing," she said.

I barely nodded.

We reached the end of the courtyard, where the instruments were set up for the performers. There would be a steady rotation of music all night long. African drummers, a rock band, the Old Guy's quartet . . . but we were singing first.

"You'll set the tone," Ms. Marion told us every year.

As soon as we reached her, I could tell she was upset. She was pinching the bridge of her nose again.

"Girls. Good. You're here." Her words were short and snappy.

Some of the other choir members were milling around, and Keisha waved at Khalil, wiggling her fingers down low, near her hip, like it was a secret just between the two of them. I scanned the crowd for Kenny, but there was no sign of him.

I told myself that was no big deal, but I couldn't help wishing he might appear at my side and take my hand again. I wondered what it would feel like if Kenny never came back to choir. Would his mother pull him out because of the shooting? How could I miss someone I'd hardly talked to before?

"Is it nearly time?" I asked Ms. Marion. I didn't have a watch, and I was hoping it was still early, since only about half the choir had shown up.

"It's six fifteen," Ms. Marion said as her whole body drooped onto a metal folding chair. "How am I s'posed to keep this up?" she asked, shaking her head. "I imagine you children leading by example, making beautiful music together, but how can I keep this going when the devil steals half my choir? *Half.*"

For a moment I thought Ms. Marion might cry, and that thought scared me deep in my bones. If Ms. Marion cried, I knew it would be a flood of tears, like after Hurricane Katrina, when my whole neighborhood had been forced to evacuate. I was too young to remember, but you could still see the water marks on some of the buildings.

Ms. Marion stood up.

"Well," she said, "I guess God never said He was going to make things easy, now did He? But we're going to do what we always do, which is to band together and sing our hearts out. Can you do that for me, Tia?"

I nodded. More than anything, I wanted to make things better for Ms. Marion.

"Choir! Assemble!" Ms. Marion called, holding up her arms. Her voice boomed into the evening air, and one by one, kids emerged. I stepped onto the lowest riser and started a weak hum to warm up my vocal cords.

Mary-Kate brushed past me. "I can't believe you showed up," she hissed, tossing her long brown curls over her shoulder. "That's nervy. Considering."

She stepped away before I had a chance to respond, taking her place on the top riser, and I could feel her eyes burning into me. I wondered how she'd found out. Had her mother told her last night, the way Ms. Evette had told Keisha? Or had she known all along? Was that the real reason she'd always hated me?

My knees were weak. Straight ahead of me, Ms. Marion was addressing the crowd, talking about loss and what it means to be a community.

"When bad things happen," she said, "we must pull together and focus on the goodness all around us, like these beautiful children who will bless us tonight with the power of their music."

The audience clapped, but I felt the *how-could-she-show-up* underneath their applause.

"And now," Ms. Marion said, "the Rainbow Choir will perform in honor of the child that was taken too soon from this world. Our first selection, 'I Know,' features our lead soloist, the talented Tia Rose Frank." She turned and motioned for me to step forward.

Everyone waited, but I couldn't move. In the evening sunlight, I could see all the eyes staring at me, and I imagined each person wishing I hadn't come, wondering what right I, of all people, had to sing in honor of a murdered baby.

"Tia," Ms. Marion said, her brows crinkling. "Whenever you're ready."

The audience shuffled nervously, and I saw people whispering to one another. A man scowled and then spat on the ground, and several teenagers laughed. My heart was pounding, my palms were sweating, and the silence stretched on, taut as a rubber band about to snap.

But no matter how hard I tried to move, I remained frozen in place.

Finally, I shook my head.

That's when I heard a voice above me. "I can sing the

lead, Ms. Marion." It was Mary-Kate. I glanced up at her fake angelic smile and knew she was stealing my part.

But I didn't care.

She could have all of my beautiful colored scarves. I didn't deserve them.

Ms. Marion looked at me, concerned, but finally she gestured for Mary-Kate to move down front.

"Ms. Mary-Kate Torelo," Ms. Marion said to the crowd, sweeping her hand in a dramatic arc. The band started up, and when Mary-Kate began to sing, I tasted the salty tears sneaking past my lips.

Without any warning, I was four years old again, visiting my father in prison, strung tight with fear and grief. I remembered his unruly hair, so like mine, his high forehead, hollow cheeks, and dark stubble. Tattoos peeked out from the collar of his orange jumpsuit, and his upper lip rose into a sneer when he saw that Ma had brought me.

"Don't be bringing her here."

I'd hid behind Ma, but he'd glared straight at me.

"Look kid," he'd said, "it ain't your fault you've got a trucker for a dad. Last thing you need is to go through *this* crap." He'd gestured around the big room where all the inmates were visiting their families, but I'd known he meant the other part—the scary part where we'd had to get searched by a security guard and go through two sets of doors that locked with a loud clang behind us.

Ma had covered my ears when my father said he was a trucker, but I'd still heard her growl, "You're an ungrateful fool, Lyle Frank."

I'd been so busy wondering why my father had claimed to be a truck driver when he'd never worked a steady job in his life that I hadn't said anything, and by the time Ma's hands had fallen off my ears, they were deep in a full-on fight. Years later I'd realized my dad hadn't said trucker after all. He'd said a real bad word instead, and I'd wanted to ask Ma why he'd said that, but if I even mentioned someone with the same first name as my dad, Ma would be in bed with a migraine for days.

Now the whole memory came back and all I could do was take deep, rhythmic breaths while Mary-Kate Torelo belted out the lead.

When she was done, everyone clapped and whistled, and Mary-Kate bowed. Ms. Marion cued our next song, and the choir began to sway, but I'd had enough. I slipped off the risers and into the crowd, walking straight back to the far corner.

I wanted to be alone—possibly forever—but a little while later, I felt a hand on my arm. "You feeling okay?" Dwayne asked.

I nodded as if my insides weren't churning up.

"Just got nervous," I mumbled as the choir sang in the background. "Stage fright."

Dwayne raised one eyebrow. "*You* got stage fright?"

I nodded again, and Dwayne folded his arms across his chest, frowning like he was thinking real hard. "You know what I like about you, Tia?" he asked at last.

I shook my head, chewing on my bottom lip.

"I like that you're a terrible liar. You know why?"

"No."

"Because," he said, "it means you're good at heart."

Dwayne reached out one large, strong hand and despite all the darkness inside of me, I took hold. It was as if there was a war going on, and his little bit of good had swooped in at the last minute to save the day.

That made me think about my father. Would any part of him care that I loved Dwayne more than him? Would he be happy that I'd remembered him tonight, or sad that I'd forgotten him in the first place? Did he remember *me*?

"C'mon," Dwayne said once the choir had finished. "Looks like my princess has found herself a prince." He nodded toward Keisha and Khalil coming off the risers, holding hands as they slipped into the crowd. "So I guess we minions might as well go find the queen."

He meant Ms. Evette, and he was trying to make me laugh, but I couldn't do it. Not tonight. Dusk was creeping in, the fireflies were coming out, and the sky was streaked with the remnants of a New Orleans sunset, but all I could think about was my father's face as he'd watched me and Ma walk out of the visiting room that last time.

He'd looked like the Raven woman. As if he'd lost something he could never get back, and part of him had died too.

That thought made me shiver.

Was that what it felt like to live behind bars, knowing you'd never again feel a cool breeze at night or watch fireflies light up the darkness? Knowing that your child would grow up without you, reaching out for a father's hand that could never be yours?

CHAPTER 11

WHEN I GOT home, the house was dark, and I knew Ma was already in bed. Ms. Evette, Dwayne, Jerome, and Keisha saw me to my door, and Keisha hugged me before she left. She'd talked about Khalil the whole way home—how gorgeous and smart and talented he is—but now she frowned.

"Sorry about tonight," she said. "Guess I was wrong about no one else knowing about your dad. Are you mad I didn't hang out with you?"

I shook my head. "I'm just glad you and Khalil had a good time."

She grinned like a lit sparkler. "We did. He's so amazing."

"Tell me more about it tomorrow?"

Keisha nodded, and I was relieved to slip away. When I stepped inside, I triple-locked the door, checking the chain twice before I shut off the outside lights. Ma had left a plate of food with a note in the kitchen, but I still couldn't eat, so I stuck it in the refrigerator. Then I went into my bedroom and put on my softest pajamas: the ones with the yellow stars that I'd mostly outgrown.

It was strange the way my body was growing, but I still felt the same. Sometimes I wanted to stay me forever, never wanted to outgrow my old star pajamas, but other times I was so scared of getting left behind. Keisha had already started her period, but I hadn't. What if mine never came?

I wondered if Danielle had ever gotten her period, but it felt wrong to wonder about such a personal thing. Still . . . did she ever have a boyfriend? A best friend? What had she wanted to be when she grew up?

Made me feel lonely, so I went into Ma's room and climbed into bed with her, squeezing next to her thin frame. Hours later, I finally fell asleep listening to the sound of her breathing, real steady, like a metronome keeping the beat.

∾

When I woke, Ma was already up and the mattress felt too big. I rolled around for a few minutes, then got up, and went into the kitchen. Ma was in her bathrobe standing at the sink doing dishes, but when I came out she stopped, walked over, and kissed me on the forehead.

"How did it go last night?"

Horrible. The worst night ever.

"Tia? I asked you a question."

"What?" I glanced up. "Good."

Ma nodded, as if *good* were enough information. "Now, what do you want for our feast?"

Saturday morning feasts were our tradition. Ma went to work at the grocery store later on Saturdays, so we cooked a huge breakfast and stayed in our pajamas for as long as possible.

"Waffles?" she prompted. "And maybe some orange slices and sausages?"

I opened my mouth to tell her that I didn't feel like having a feast today, but Ma was already getting her old CD player down from the top of the refrigerator. No one else I knew listened to CDs, but Ma still used the same player she'd had since I was a baby. She put on Nanci Griffith, her favorite bluegrass singer. Usually I sang along and Ma would listen and smile. Sometimes she hummed and every now and then she'd break into a line of song, as if she didn't realize what she was doing. But now we were quiet as she cracked the eggs into the flour and sugar. She always took the time to make the waffles from scratch.

What would she say when I told her that I knew what my father had done? I wanted to scream at her for not telling me everything, but how could I yell at someone who worked every spare minute to keep us from falling apart?

Ma stopped and wiped her forehead with the back of her arm. She looked exhausted. Other people had hobbies, or at least they watched TV shows—*something*—but Ma had nothing except two jobs and Saturday mornings.

Finally, I couldn't stand it.

"Sit down, Ma," I said. "Let me finish up."

Ma paused, looking between me and the waffle maker, but she didn't argue. "Be sure to spray it extra good," she said, sitting down at the kitchen table and propping her slippered feet onto a chair. I nodded and took two plates out of the cupboard. I peeled an orange and pulled apart the segments, their fragrance squirting into the air in a light orange mist. I chewed my bottom lip, wondering what I should say.

"Ma," I said at last.

"Yes?"

"Do you think we could talk about . . . the past? I mean . . . about—"

All the color drained from Ma's face. Her feet slid off the chair and she looked like she might be sick. I could see the pinch around her eyes that happened right before a migraine hit.

"I meant, could we look at your old pictures?"

Ma's breath released in a whoosh of relief. "Again?" she said, cracking a thin smile.

"It's been a long time," I argued, forcing the words out even as my heart broke. "And I want to see the ones of Grammy and Grandpa."

Ma stood up. "You gotta use more spray than that," she said, watching over my shoulder. "Sure. I'll go get the box."

Ma kept all her photos in a shoebox under her bed. They were worn and bent in places from us looking at them so often. She disappeared for a second, then came back and set the box onto the table while I finished up the waffles.

I really did like looking at the pictures, so before I knew it, I was as caught up as Ma. We riffled through the box while we ate, taking our time examining each photo between syrupy bites, wiping our fingertips on washcloths, and being extra careful not to let the syrup drip.

I loved the pictures of Ma as a teenager. She was usually posing with her hip jutted to one side or her mouth in a pout. Her hair was teased high on her head, and Ma laughed about how much hairspray she'd used to make it stay up. She looked so beautiful in those pictures—light and free, like all she did was laugh.

Hard to imagine.

I wondered if there was a picture of my father in that box, but I'd never dared to ask. Ma rooted around until she found a photo of her parents. They stood in front of their house on Felicity Street, Grandpa with a big, round belly and Grammy with a stick-thin frame. Grandpa smiled like someone had just told a joke, and Grammy's eyes sparkled.

I wished I had known them. Grandpa died not long after

Ma graduated from high school, so I'd never met him, and Grammy passed away when I was small.

"They were so kind," Ma said. "Your grandmother sang like an angel. You sound just like her. Sometimes when I close my eyes . . ." Ma breathed in deep. "I love it when you sing," she said, "even if I don't always make it to your concerts. You know that, right? I bet you were spectacular last night."

I tightened my hands into fists and felt my heart racing, too fast and too hard. Ma didn't even know I hadn't sung.

"Ma," I blurted, "tell me about my father."

Ma had been sipping orange juice, but now she choked on it. She coughed the way people do when something has gone down the wrong pipe, hacking so hard I thought she might throw up.

"No," Ma said between coughs.

She stood up and took her plate to the sink. She was still for a long time, leaning against the counter, and then she closed her eyes. "This isn't a good time. I have to get dressed for my shift." She was angry. "You could have given me some warning."

"Please." How could Ma and I share the same secret without ever talking about it?

"No," Ma said again. "I've told you before, there's no point in bringing up the past. You know all there is to know."

Another lie.

I watched Ma disappear into her room to put her uniform

on, knowing that when she came out, her shoulders would be slumped and her eyes would be flat. She emerged a while later, set for work. For a few minutes she bustled around the kitchen without saying anything, and then she stepped up to the front door. "I'm pulling a double tonight," she said, one hand on the doorknob, "so don't wait up."

Guilt made my stomach churn.

I'd spoiled the only time all week when she was happy.

CHAPTER 12

ONCE MA was gone, the house was quiet.

I tossed my dishes into the sink with a loud clatter, not sure who I was more frustrated with: me or Ma. Why wouldn't she tell me the truth? And why couldn't I make her?

I kicked at a bag of foam peanuts, spilling some onto the floor, then picked up the shoebox and turned it upside down. Pictures flew everywhere, fluttering across the linoleum. I watched them fall, wanting to stomp on them, but instead I knelt and picked them up one by one, placing them back in the box.

There had to be a picture of my father in there. Just one.

I'd seen most of the photos a hundred times, but a few were unfamiliar—the ones Ma kept stashed at the bottom. But none of them were of him.

Where was he?

Ma had married him, they'd had me, we'd been a family, lived together in this very house. Was it possible that a person could be absent from an entire lifetime of photographs? I grabbed the box and hurled it across the kitchen.

When it landed, the pictures I'd just put back spilled out and one of them slid under the refrigerator. I grabbed the yardstick, got down on my hands and knees, and guided it out, and that's when I saw the second photo. It was a three-by-five color snapshot of my parents sitting on the steps of their high school. My father, his dark hair trimmed short, was laughing, one arm around my freckle-faced mother, pulling her close. Ma was looking up at him, smiling so big, I hardly recognized her. And he was looking back, grinning as if he'd never seen anyone so beautiful.

I stared at the photo.

Where was the evil? This person had ended up committing murder and had gone to jail for life. Shouldn't badness be something you could see coming?

Yet, here he was.

My father.

Happy.

~

Dwelling has a way of muddling time. One minute it's early and you have the whole day ahead of you, and the next, that day is drifting away. I stared at the photograph of my father, trying to decide what I should do with it. I decided to go to Keisha's house, figuring maybe I'd show her the picture. But when I walked out, instead of turning toward her place, I went left, toward the baby's house.

I thought about the Raven woman's face in the window, and I couldn't help wondering if she'd ever feel happy again. Maybe she'd smile and laugh, but wouldn't there always be something missing? Years from now, when she looked through her photos, would she ache for the ones that weren't there?

When I got to the house, it was quiet and still, and I guessed right away that it was empty. I supposed that made sense. There were probably all sorts of baby things inside. Reminders of how unlivable life could be.

I thought about turning around, but I didn't.

Sweat dripped down my back, and the soft blue T-shirt and shorts I'd pulled on that morning clung to my skin. I realized my hands were clenched tight, and the imprints of my fingers made deep red grooves in my palms. They stung as I unclasped them. I sat down beside the memorial fence, pulling my bare knees into my chest. After a long while, I took the photo of my father out of the pocket of my shorts.

All that happiness, ruined.

I remembered Danielle Morton's huge smile. She'd had no idea that she would end up murdered. Did her family and friends still miss her every day, even after eight years had gone by?

I wanted to rip the photo to shreds, but I couldn't do it.

This was the only picture I had. Even if Ma had kept another one, it wasn't like I could ask her for it. Then again, maybe my father didn't deserve to be remembered.

I studied the memorial fence. The candles had been knocked over, and some of the teddy bears had fallen down, so I set my father's photo on the sidewalk and walked over. I straightened each item, then retied a sagging ribbon closer to the iron filigree. A section of chain link had been set up to hold messages and photographs, but it had slumped, so I stood it upright and plugged some of the cards, handwritten prayers, and small crosses deeper into the holes where people had wedged them.

Trash was scattered in the yard—small bits of wrapping and debris. I gathered each piece, slowly and meticulously, and set them in the trash can by the side of the house. Then I swept the sidewalk with a broken broom that had been sitting beside the door. The handle was cracked in the middle, so it took me a long time. All the while, the sun was hot on my back and my hair loosed itself from my elastic and fell into my face.

A soft hitching noise made me look up, and that's when I saw the Raven woman standing in her doorway. A long black skirt billowed around her legs, blowing in the breeze.

Our eyes met and my heart skipped a beat.

At first I thought she might turn around and go back inside, but instead she walked down the few steps to the sidewalk and opened her front gate. It creaked on rusty hinges, the sound piercing the humid air. She came over and crouched beside me, reaching for a stuffed elephant that had gotten ground into the mud at the bottom of the fence. Ever so carefully, she brushed the dirt off its soft gray surface. Then she touched her finger to her tongue, rubbing the elephant's tiny glass eyes.

"There," she said, in an accent so thick, I could hardly make out the word. "Now it will be . . ." She seemed to search her mind. "Best?"

I nodded blankly.

I might have said a million different things, but the woman reached out and touched my hair, her fingers trailing a long, unruly strand.

"Pretty," she said, smiling sadly.

"Thank you," I whispered.

Her eyes were red-rimmed and she looked tired. I wondered how she'd managed to get out of bed, and I was about to say something about being sorry for what had happened, but then she did something I didn't expect.

She reached out and picked up the photo of my father.

"No," I sputtered. "Don't."

My hand grabbed for hers, but she brushed me aside. Carefully, she hung my father's picture on the fence between a photo of her son and a hand-painted sign that read LOVE NEVER DIES.

"Please," I pleaded. "He shouldn't be up there."

I reached out, but the woman stopped my hand.

"Stay," she said firmly.

She patted my hand twice as if to ensure that I wouldn't remove my father's photo, and then she turned and walked up the steps. I watched her pause at her door and look back at me with a knowing, exhausted look. She thought I was grieving, like her. I couldn't let her think that, but how could I tell her the truth?

At last, she disappeared inside, leaving me to stare at my father's picture, knowing he was looking back at me from the last place he belonged.

CHAPTER 13

MONDAY MORNING, I sat at the kitchen table stealing glances at the Sunday paper, which Ma had brought home a day late. She could take papers for free if there were leftovers, and she always brought a stack for wrapping stuff.

There was an article about the baby. **POLICE ANNOUNCE LEADS**. Above the article was a picture of the baby's mother at the funeral, sagging into the arms of the people supporting her on either side. Her face was turned up to the sky as if she were sending God an ocean of fury.

Maybe God deserved her anger. Or maybe the person who did the carjacking deserved it and God was getting a raw deal. I didn't know.

I closed my eyes and breathed deep, but Ma interrupted, her voice stern.

"Tia, your toast is getting cold." Ma came over and shut the paper with a slap. Then she threw it into an empty box, and carried the box to her bedroom.

"I was reading that," I called after her, but she didn't answer, just came back and sat down across from me. I thought for sure she was going to say something about my father. She was finally going to tell me everything. I took a deep breath, my chest tightening, willing it to happen.

"Want to play Scrabble?"

What?

"Uh, I-I," I stammered. "I guess so?"

"Great."

Ma got up and took the game out of the hall closet, then set up the worn board I'd picked up at a yard sale. Ma drew the tile with the most points, so she went first. She took her time studying the letters, then placed them on the board.

M-U-T-E

I drew in my breath. Had she done that on purpose or was it a coincidence?

My hand hesitated above my tiles. I had a blank one, which I used as a V to make E-V-A-D-E. The word had been on my vocabulary list last year in English.

Ma pursed her lips, taking a long time before putting her next word down on a double letter score. E-A-R-N

Earn? What the heck did that mean? A surge of fury washed over me. Didn't make any sense to be angry about a Scrabble word, but I couldn't help it. I didn't have good letters, so all I could do was place an O next to her N to make N-O.

Ma made a huffing noise. "That's not much of a word," she chided. "You can't do any better than that? Doesn't leave me much to work with."

"This is a game," I snapped. "Why should I help you win?"

Ma's eyes shot up, and she raised an eyebrow at me. For a long moment, the two of us sat there with our eyes locked, and then Ma scowled and made M-A-D.

To which I added N-E-S-S.

M-A-D-N-E-S-S. "Double word score," I said.

Ma shook her head. I couldn't decide if she was angry or not, but then she used my S to make Y-I-P-E-S

"Yipes?"

"It's in the Scrabble dictionary," Ma said. "You can check if you want to."

I stood up. "I don't want to play after all."

"Okay," Ma said, frowning. For a long time, neither of us said anything, but finally Ma sighed. "Maybe we could do something else."

"Like what?" I asked, sinking into our living room couch and crossing my arms over my chest. Right then, I didn't want to do anything with Ma ever again, but then she said the one thing I couldn't resist.

"Like . . . maybe we could bake that woman some bread."

I looked up quick, sure that I must have heard her wrong. "What did you say?"

"The woman in the newspaper," Ma said. "She and her

husband live around here. Sometimes when people are grieving, other people bring them meals." Ma paused. "I suppose it's awkward, but—"

"Please," I interrupted. "Let's do it."

Ma sat still, like she was already regretting her offer. "Bread takes time," she warned. "It's not quick and easy the way cakes and cookies are . . . not if you make it from scratch. You have to mix the dough, then knead it and punch it down, then let it rise, knead it and punch it down again. It'll take us all day, and you know I've got to nap since I'm working the night shift tonight."

"You can nap while the dough is rising," I said, trying not to sound too eager.

Ma walked into the kitchen, opening cupboards, searching for ingredients.

"I don't even know if they'll want something from—well, if they'll want it. But we could leave it in their mailbox if it would help you to stop dwelling."

I nodded. "It would."

Ma pulled items out, one by one. Flour, sugar, salt, baking powder.

I walked over and hugged Ma tight.

"Thanks," I said, but Ma just shook her head.

"Don't thank me yet. We've still got all the work to do."

~

Ma was right about baking bread. It really did take all day, but by evening our house smelled so good, I thought I might burst. We'd made three braided loaves: one for the baby's family, one for us, and one for Ms. Evette. Plus, we'd made a dozen clover leaf rolls from the extra dough. Ma and I had eaten ours hot out of the oven with melted butter and a dusting of cinnamon, and I had more rolls wrapped in a dishtowel next to the braided bread we were taking to Keisha's. I held the whole package in my arms and it warmed me straight through.

Every Monday night I slept over at Keisha's while Ma worked the overnight shift. Ma walked me there before she went to work, and then on Tuesday morning, Ms. Evette walked me to my lesson with Ms. Marion before she caught the streetcar. It was a perfectly coordinated schedule that we'd kept every summer for years, but now all I could think about was dropping off that warm, crusty bread.

"Can we bring it over right now?" I asked.

Ma paused a moment too long.

"There isn't time," she said. "I'll drop it off on my way home."

"But couldn't we just . . ."

Ma's eyes flashed. "No back-talk, young lady."

I wanted to argue that I hadn't been back-talking, but we'd had a fun day baking, so I didn't want to ruin things with a fight.

"Sorry," I said at last. "It's just . . . you won't forget, will you?"

Ma's face relaxed. She took the bread off the counter and placed it inside the big canvas bag she carried to and from work. "I won't forget." Then she leaned over and kissed me on top of the head. "You did something real nice today, Tia girl. Now you've got to let the adults handle the rest, you hear?"

I felt the warm rolls pressed up against my body. Slowly, I nodded.

"Promise?"

Could it be that easy?

"I promise."

Ma let out a long, loud breath. Louder, I bet, than she'd intended.

"Good," she said. "That's real good."

That night, me and Keisha, Ms. Evette, Dwayne, and Jerome ate fresh clover leaf rolls with our pork chops and greens. Jerome said, "Mo, mo, mo," and pointed at the bread, and we cut into it even though Ms. Evette had said we were going to save the loaf for breakfast. Everyone mmmm'ed until I blushed, and Dwayne said I could cook for him anytime.

After dinner me and Keisha watched *The Next American Superstar.* We draped ourselves over the couch and plotted how we'd convince people that we were old enough to audition when the show came back to New Orleans. Dwayne was giving Jerome his bath in the next room and I could hear the sound of splashing.

Keisha was hanging upside down off the side of the couch, but she sat up when the commercials came on. "You know," she said to her mother, "we need to enter all sorts of contests if we're going to make it big. How else will we get discovered? Khalil and his friends are putting together a band and they're going to audition when *The Next American Superstar* comes back to town."

Ms. Evette was sitting in the beige easy chair, under the tall lamp, carving a baby bird for a necklace. She barely looked up. "Mmm-hmm."

Dwayne came out carrying a soaking wet Jerome, bundled in a thick towel, and Keisha and I both kissed his sopping brown curls.

"Night-night," we said, and Jerome waved.

Dwayne handed him over to Ms. Evette, who reluctantly put down her whittling to get him into his pj's and read him books before bed.

"Dad," Keisha said when her mother was gone, "do you think Tia and I could enter some contests? We've got to become famous while we're still young and cute."

Dwayne's face went blank.

"What are you talking about?" he said. "You mean you're not superstars already? Not a one of you is famous yet?"

Keisha giggled and I grinned.

Dwayne shook his head. "Because I thought you were. I mean, I hear you two doing your *top secret* handshake all the time, and—"

"Dad!"

"—I hear you all singing away upstairs."

Dwayne twirled around with one hand in the air, jutting his hips from side to side. "Like a pyramid, oh, I'm a pyramid," he sang in a crazy high falsetto. "Got my pretty bow in my hair, and my tight jeans on—"

Keisha tackled him around the waist and the two of them fell laughing into a heap on the floor. I laughed too, and for one crazy moment I imagined it was *my* father there, laughing and tickling, singing in falsetto and dishing up the love.

CHAPTER 14

THE NEXT MORNING the apartment was quiet. Dwayne wasn't up yet, Keisha was still in her pajamas, and Ms. Evette, Jerome, and I were sitting around the kitchen table eating thick slabs of toasted bread with strawberry jam. Jerome had jam all over him—even in his ear. Ms. Evette was reading the morning paper and she didn't look happy.

"Says here they've arrested two young men for that carjacking," she grumbled. "'Course it's two black men, so who knows if they've got the right people or they've just got the most *convenient* people."

She set the paper down with a shove and sipped her coffee. I was burning to look at the article, wondering if there might be pictures of the men and whether I'd see the bad in their eyes. But I forced myself to sit still and wait until she was done. When I finally got a look at the paper, there weren't any pictures at all. Just two names: *Tarik Miller, 29,* and *Rondo Waters, 24.* Who were they? Did they have families? Kids?

“Do you know how many African American men are falsely imprisoned each year?” Ms. Evette was saying. “Too many. Precious young men, stolen from this community. It’s a shame.”

From the living room, I heard Keisha groan. “Ma,” she complained, “it’s too early for this lecture. I haven’t even had breakfast yet.”

“That’s not my fault,” Ms. Evette scolded. “Get dressed, get your butt in the kitchen, and eat something.”

Keisha shuffled in, rubbing her eyes. Jerome tossed a bit of toast onto the floor and she leaned over to pick it up, tickling him under his chin.

“You’re such a stinker,” she said as Jerome tossed more toast.

Ms. Evette watched them, and at first her face was still hard and grumbly, but then she smiled as Jerome put a bit of soggy toast in Keisha’s mouth and Keisha sputtered, spitting it out real fast. Ms. Evette chuckled, and it was as if I could see the exact moment she’d moved on from the news.

“Come on,” she said, cleaning Jerome off with a washcloth and then lifting him up from his high chair. “Time to catch the streetcar.” She nodded to me. “Let’s get moving, hon. Keisha, you eat something healthy. And don’t play your music too loud. Your dad’s sleeping.”

Dwayne had been out of work for a long time, but sometimes he was able to pick up a night shift at the Autocenter. They paid him cash under the table so he wouldn't lose his unemployment.

Keisha nodded and I sighed, thinking about my lesson with Ms. Marion. Normally, I couldn't wait, but I was dreading this one. I knew she'd have something to say about me handing my lead over to Mary-Kate at June Fest.

I said good-bye to Keisha as Ms. Evette put on Jerome's tiny sneakers and grabbed her briefcase. Then I followed them out of the apartment and down the steps. It was bright and sunny, and a cool breeze made the banana trees wave. We walked real quiet for a couple blocks before Ms. Evette glanced my way.

"I've missed your singing," she said. "You've been some quiet these past few days."

"I have?" I said, as if I hadn't felt the loss like a punch to the gut. Singing was my favorite thing in the world, so why didn't I want to do it anymore?

Ms. Evette laughed. "Okay," she said. "You be that way if you must, but just remember that I'm not so senile yet that I don't remember what it was like to be your age. Lots of changes going on."

I blushed, knowing she meant stuff like having crushes on boys and wearing a bra.

"I know," I said, trying not to stare at the spot where the car had been.

"Good," said Ms. Evette, stopping in front of the New Heaven Baptist Church. "Now you open up and sing in there, you hear? And be careful walking home."

I pushed a dried palm frond on the sidewalk with the toe of my sneaker.

"I will," I mumbled, and then I reached up and put my fingertip on Jerome's because he was pointing at me as if he wanted to tell me something. "Bye-bye," I told him, before ducking into the church building.

The inside of the New Heaven Baptist Church was musty and dark. The stained-glass windows didn't let in any real light, so whenever I stepped inside, it felt like another world. I was glad Ms. Marion lived too far away to do lessons in her home like other teachers. Even after everything that had happened, I still loved the dark wood pews and red velvet seat cushions. I loved the smallness of the sanctuary and the closeness of the pulpit. Felt like you could see everything there was to see, so there would be no surprises.

Except it hadn't worked out that way, had it?

Ms. Marion was waiting for me up front, like always, and my stomach clenched. I walked down the center aisle real slow and when I reached the piano, I made a show of finding the envelope with her payment in it.

Ms. Marion looked me over, top to bottom, and I waited for her to tell me how disappointed she'd been in me at June

Fest, and how the choir had been depending on me and I'd let everyone down. I waited for the lecture about how great singers never gave up, even when life was hard.

Ms. Marion paused. "Tia, how's your mama?"

That was the last thing I was expecting. My eyes opened wide. "Good, I guess," I said. "Same as always."

"I see," said Ms. Marion. "Didn't she go to church here a long time ago? Evette tells me they used to be in the choir together."

I shook my head. "Not here," I corrected. "They sang together in their high school choir."

"Ahh. And does she still sing?"

"No, ma'am."

"How about your father?" Ms. Marion asked. "Does he sing?"

I just about choked on my own spit.

"He's . . . he's in . . . prison," I sputtered.

Ms. Marion nodded. "I know, child," she said. "But even in prison, people can still sing."

She might as well have said the sky was purple.

Ms. Marion raised one eyebrow. "Would you like to talk about your father?"

I didn't answer. My stomach was too busy doing somersaults.

Ms. Marion nodded like she'd figured out something important. "You see what happened there? First, you had a voice, talking to me and answering my questions, and then that voice just disappeared, didn't it?"

Ms. Marion took my hands in hers. "You know something, Tia?" she said. "You are the best singer in the entire choir. In fact, you're the most naturally talented child I have ever met."

I looked up quick, and she smiled.

"Don't tell the others I said so, but it's true. Out of that skinny little body of yours comes a sound so large, it gives me goose bumps. But I think you've got yourself blocked up, am I right? Saw it happen with my own eyes."

Shame crawled up my neck, and Ms. Marion sighed.

"Have you done any singing since last Thursday?"

I shook my head and felt the tears welling up in the corners of my eyes.

"And I bet you think if you could only get your mind to stop churning, everything would be fine, wouldn't it?"

I swallowed hard, thinking about my father and Danielle, and how all I'd been doing was dwelling on the miserable facts.

"Ms. Marion?" I asked. "Do you believe in the stuff we sing about? I mean, about God being good and people going to heaven when they die? Do you think those songs are true, or did the people who wrote them just not know about all the bad things that happen in the world?"

Ms. Marion held up one hand.

"Oh, child," she said, "you can't imagine all of what those people knew." She took a deep breath. "Most of what we sing is gospel. Do you know where gospel music comes from?"

I shook my head.

"Started with slavery," Ms. Marion said. "Imagine you were taken from your home and your family and everything you knew, and all you had left was your memories and your music. Think how that music would bubble up out of your soul." Ms. Marion took a breath in through her nostrils and then she sang.

Deep river, my home is over Jordan,
Deep river, Lord, I want to cross over into campground,
Oh, don't you want to go to that gospel feast,
That promised land where all is peace?

"Slaves would sing as they worked in the fields, and little by little the Christian message made its way into those songs. Lord knows how anything beautiful could have come out of those troubled times, but it sure did." She shook her head. "It sure did."

I thought that over. "So do you think they believed it?" I asked. "The good parts, I mean?"

Ms. Marion scratched her chin. "Well, you're talking about millions of people. I'm sure some of them sang out of hope, and some of them sang just to make the time tolerable. But what matters is what *you* believe."

"What if I don't know?"

Ms. Marion lifted my chin. "'Course you don't know," she said. "You've got to work it out."

My heart sunk, but Ms. Marion shook her head. "As for me? I don't think the world is a bad place. And I don't think a person can be completely bad either."

That caught me off guard, but Ms. Marion held me still with her eyes.

"You know, sometimes if you're having trouble creating something beautiful, you've got to find the joy in your life. Focus on the good things." She sighed. "But I know that's easier said than done."

I thought about gunshots piercing the air and a girl my age who'd never get to grow up. But then I thought about Dwayne's firm hand at June Fest and Jerome covered in strawberry jam. Saturday morning feasts and favorite songs that could still make me smile.

Ms. Marion handed me back the envelope with Ma's money in it. "Here's what we're going to do. I'm going to give you time to figure this out. I won't expect you at lessons until you're ready. Come to rehearsals and listen in, but we'll tell everyone you're having throat problems. If you need me, you know where to find me."

I was torn between disappointment and relief. I hated missing even one lesson, but for the first time in days I felt as if I might be able to sing again. I stuck the envelope in my pocket, thinking that Ma would never admit it, but she'd be glad to have that money back.

"Thank you, Ms. Marion."

Ms. Marion gathered up her things. "Well, go on then," she said, nodding for me to head out.

Reluctantly, I left the enclosure of the dark church, moving out into the sun, then through the shade, and finally into the sun again. The whole time I saw myself as if from above, moving through the shadows and the sunshine, unsure if I'd ever come to a stop, but hoping I'd land in the light.

CHAPTER 15

AFTER LESSONS I'm supposed to go straight home. Ma is back from work by then and if I'm even five minutes late, she's got the phone in her hand ready to dial 911. But today I'd gotten out early.

I thought about the bread Ma had promised to drop off and decided I'd be brave and write a note to go with it. I wasn't sure what I'd say. Maybe just something plain, like you'd find in a card. *Sorry for your loss.* I guessed it didn't really matter. What could words say, anyway? The point was that you wrote them.

I wondered if the bread would still be in the metal mailbox outside the front door. Ma would've had to leave it there. Wasn't any place else suitable. We'd wrapped it in layer upon layer of tin foil, so I supposed she could have left it by the front door, but I didn't guess Ma would do that. I just hoped no one had come by to collect it already.

When I arrived, there was an old lady at the top of the

steps. She wore a long black dress, and her wrinkled face sagged.

I stopped short.

She was pulling things out of the mailbox: slim white envelopes, square colored cards, and small packages. When it was empty, she bent to pick up a basket someone had left on the stoop. It was filled with cookies and flowers, and for a moment I thought maybe Ma had put our bread in there, but I could see there wasn't a loaf inside. I opened the wrought-iron gate and stepped into the yard as the old lady watched me from the top step.

"Excuse me," I said, real polite, "my mother left a loaf of homemade bread here, and I wanted to write a note to go with it, if that's okay."

The woman looked confused, and I began to feel prickly.

"Did you find some bread?" I asked, more slowly. "Here on the step or in the mailbox?"

The old woman shrugged and said a stream of words I didn't recognize.

"Bread," I said again, making the size and shape of the bread loaf with my hands. I pretended to eat and then felt foolish.

The old woman tilted her head, gesturing to her full arms. "No bread."

My forehead crinkled. "But it must be there. Did you come by earlier today?"

I knew she might not understand, but I couldn't help saying the words.

"This . . . everything," the old woman said, nodding as if she was certain she'd made her point. She stepped gingerly down the first step, her arms full to overflowing, and at first I just stared at her, stunned.

The old woman stumbled, and finally I remembered my manners and offered her my arm. She handed me the basket and smiled when I took it. When she'd made it all the way down the steps, we walked together to her car. She opened the front door, and as I set the basket inside, I looked up and saw the baby's picture on the dashboard next to a small wooden cross. He was posed against one of those fake backdrops, smiling with two tiny teeth poking out of his bottom gum. He had beautiful blue eyes, pudgy cheeks, and little baby hands.

I pulled away quick.

"Sorry," I said. "I'm so sorry."

She nodded as she buckled her seat belt, and then I watched the old woman drive off before turning and walking away. This time, I didn't bother staying in the sunlight. I walked straight through the shadows without ever looking up.

Why had we bothered to bake the bread if Ma had never meant to give it away?

~

When I got back, Ma looked surprised to see me. She had her nightgown on, and I knew she was waiting for me to get home before she went to bed. She was always tired after working all night, but today I didn't care. I was boiling mad and there wasn't a single speck of room left for pity.

"You're home early," she said, looking up from her magazine.

I thrust the envelope from Ms. Marion at her. "Ms. Marion says we'll be taking a break."

Ma took the money, cocking her head to one side. "Did she say why she—"

"Did you drop off the bread?"

Ma paused. "Are you all right?"

She reached for my arm, but I pulled away.

"I'm fine. I've just been . . . running, that's all. Did you drop the bread off at the house?"

Ma laughed, but it wasn't her normal laugh. She refused to meet my eyes, and I knew for certain that our bread had ended up in the snack room at Winn-Dixie.

"Of course I did," Ma scoffed. "I said I would, didn't I?"

A thousand thoughts tumbled in my mind. I saw that little baby's innocent face. Was there something so wrong with us that we weren't even worthy of giving bread to his family?

Ma was waiting for my response, but I brushed past her and ran down the hall to my room, slamming the door behind me. I heard Ma's footsteps, and then there was a hard rapping sound on my door.

"Tia, are you going to explain yourself?"

I lay down on my bed and curled into a ball.

"Tia?" Ma knocked again. There was a pause, and then Ma said, "You'd better tell me what's the matter or—"

"I started my period."

The lie came out before I'd had time to think about it. I just wanted her to leave me alone and quit asking questions. Even through the door I could hear Ma's relief. I could hear her thinking, *Ah, that explains everything.*

Her voice softened. "Oh honey, do you want to talk about it?"

"Not now," I said, forcing out the words. "Maybe later."

Ma laughed softly.

"Definitely later," she said. "Do you need anything?"

"No."

"Well, you lay down and rest for a while, and trust me, it will get better."

Liar, I thought. *Liar. Liar. Liar.*

I might not have my period yet, but Keisha had told me all about it. "Everyone wants to make out like this is something beautiful and great," she'd said, "but really, it's annoying. I get pimples before and cramps during, but of course you've got to keep doing everything just like always, even gym class. And we're going to go through this every single month until we're old, but guys don't have to feel a single cramp *ever*? That's just plain wrong."

Even though she'd said that, I'd still wanted to start mine since it seemed like every other girl our age already had, and I'd secretly imagined the way I'd talk to Ma about it. Like we'd have some deep, shared understanding of womanhood. Now some part of me knew I'd ruined that future moment, but I didn't care.

CHAPTER 16

FOR THE REST of that week, I stayed holed up in my bedroom.

I lied to Keisha and told her I had a head cold, and I kept up my lie with Ma, telling her I had cramps and wanted to rest. She'd sat on the edge of my bed, giving me the lecture about what to do now that I was a woman, and I'd pretended to care, but as soon as she was gone, I'd shut my door again.

One night I heard her on the phone with Ms. Evette.

I suppose it's natural for her to be hormonal right now.

Was Keisha like this when she . . .

I suspect you're right, it's just sometimes I think there's something else.

If Ma knew that all I was really doing in here was dwelling, she would've kicked me out of bed so fast, I would've broken the sound barrier. The truth was, I didn't even know why Ma not delivering the bread hurt so bad. Why did I feel such deep-down shame that I couldn't even tell my best friend in the entire world what had happened?

Keisha called on Monday morning, and I could hear in her voice that she wasn't messing around. "Why'd you tell me you had a head cold when really you started your period?"

She hadn't said hello or anything.

"And you know you missed choir on Thursday, hanging out all weekend, and you haven't called me in a whole week—not even to see how it's going with Khalil. I've had bad cramps before, but you better be expelling a kidney, the way you're acting."

I groaned. "Sorry."

"Sorry? That's all you've got to say for yourself?"

"I didn't start my period," I blurted.

"What?" Keisha said. "But I heard my mom talking to your mom, and she said—"

"I lied."

There was a long pause.

"Why would you lie about something like that?"

"I don't know," I said miserably. "It just came out, and then I had to keep pretending, except I didn't want to lie to *you* about that, so I came up with another lie. And then . . ."

I heard Keisha breathing on the other end.

"And then," she repeated, like it was a statement.

"I'm really sorry."

There was no sound for a long time.

"You lied to your mother about getting your period?" Keisha repeated at last. "That's rough. Why would you *do* that?"

I wasn't sure I could explain.

"I just . . . I don't know."

Keisha huffed.

"You better hope you really do start up soon or you're going to be pretending an awful lot. You're gonna have to mark it on the calendar and everything, so you won't forget."

I sighed. "I know," I said. "It was stupid, but—"

Keisha cut me off. "Honestly?" she said. "I knew you were lying about both things. The head cold was easy because you didn't sound even a little stuffed up, but the rest of it . . . I don't know. I just knew you would've told me."

We were both quiet, and then Keisha said, "You're lucky I'm not a drama queen like Tyresha. If you had that girl for a best friend, she'd be texting up the entire choir to tell them all your secrets, and then she wouldn't speak to you for, like, six months, only later she'd finally forgive you and you'd be best friends again. Me, I just cut to the chase."

For the first time in a week, I smiled. "Keisha," I said, "no one else could ever be my best friend."

Keisha laughed. "Don't you know it," she said. "Now get your butt over here. Auntie Loretta's been visiting all week-end and you haven't even seen her yet. Mama wants us all to head out to the French Quarter together."

I'd been about to ask how things were going with Khalil, but instead I cringed. Ms. Evette's sister came down from Mississippi twice a year, all lipstick and high heels, and I dreaded every visit. When it came to Keisha's aunt, I always felt like a cockroach: small, ugly, and uninvited.

I couldn't tell Keisha that, though. She adored her aunt Loretta, and seeing as she'd just given me a pass when she could have pitched a fit, I wasn't going to mess things up now.

"Great," I said. "Just give me a minute to grab my stuff."

~

"I can't believe Ms. Marion didn't say a word about you giving up the lead at June Fest," Keisha said, leaning back in her beanbag chair. "I mean, really, not one word?"

I shrugged. "She didn't seem angry. Just said I needed time to work through things."

Keisha rolled her eyes. "That's not very helpful." She sighed, but then she straightened. "Oh, Ma said you should let her know when you got here, so we can head out."

"Okay," I said, trying not to frown. "Guess I'll say hello to Loretta too."

I headed downstairs, but stopped on the final step, listening to the hushed voices coming from the kitchen. The tone of them made my skin tingle.

"I just don't see why you're still taking care of her as if she's your own kid. Does her mother even pay you?"

That was Loretta's voice, clipped and annoyed.

A wave of fear washed over me as I heard Ms. Evette cluck her tongue.

"She's Keisha's best friend. I don't *ask* for payment."

"Oh right," Loretta snorted. "Because you have all the money in the world to feed an extra mouth, what with your husband having been out of work for two years."

"We're doing fine," Ms. Evette snapped. "Just because you feel the need to put on airs every time you visit, making my daughter think you're some kind of fashion mogul . . ."

Loretta laughed. "Oh Ettie, she does not think that. Why can't I buy Keisha something pretty? That's not putting on airs. Besides, I buy things for little Ms. White Girl too. I'd think you'd be happy about that."

"She has a name," Ms. Evette said. "And this isn't about color."

"Oh come *on,*" Loretta said, snapping the words apart like each one was a separate sentence. "You're really going to tell me that a black woman taking care of a poor little white child, practically raising her while her incompetent mama refuses to pull herself together and her worthless father rots in prison, isn't about color?"

"Don't you dare!" Ms. Evette said. "Tia is a great kid."

"I'm not saying she isn't," Loretta said. "At least so far."

"What's that supposed to mean?"

"You haven't thought it?" I could hear the click of Loretta's heels. "Her father's in prison for *murder*. You know when a child's brain forms the most neural connections? During the first three years of life. What do you think a man like that taught his kid during those years? A person has to be wrong in the head to pull the trigger on a twelve-year-old girl."

Ms. Evette was trying to talk over her sister. "Tia's a child, for goodness' sake. She's not some evil spawn."

"I'm not saying you shouldn't be kind to her," Loretta answered, "I'm just saying that if I were you, I wouldn't want to keep taking care of her once she's a teenager. One way or another, that girl is going to be disturbed."

I clapped my hand over my mouth. *Was this what people thought of me?*

That's when Dwayne came around the corner. As he passed, I dashed up the stairs, hoping he hadn't seen me hovering there. I heard the low, angry thrum of his voice, but couldn't concentrate on the words. Not anymore. I darted into Keisha's room, shutting the door tight behind me.

"What's wrong?" Keisha asked. "Did you find Ma and Aunt Loretta?"

My mind raced. Should I tell Keisha what I'd heard?

Make some excuse to go home? Go downstairs and stand up for myself? My heart was *pounding, pounding, pounding*.

A second later Dwayne opened Keisha's door.

"Are you girls ready to go?"

"Don't we look ready?" Keisha asked, twirling in front of the mirror.

Dwayne frowned. "You know we're going for beignets, right? You're going to get powdered sugar all over that nice shirt." He narrowed his eyes at me. "You all right?"

I nodded, trying to breathe normally, but Dwayne's face fell, and he gave me a look so pained I wanted to shrivel up into a tiny ball. "Oh kiddo," he said. "You didn't hear that, did you?"

I looked away.

Finally, he laid one hand gently on my arm. "No matter what anyone says, you're a part of this family and we love you. Hold your chin up high, understand?" He said it real stern, searching out my gaze, and I nodded, but nothing felt real anymore. Keisha turned around and gave Dwayne a strange look, but he just squeezed my arm tight. Then he walked out, pulling the door shut behind him.

"What was that all about?" Keisha asked.

"Guess he can tell I've been upset lately."

Keisha nodded. "Forget about your stupid father," she

said. “It’s not your fault he did something terrible. No one blames *you* for it.”

But Keisha was completely and utterly wrong. For the first time, I understood why my mother had kept the truth from me for all these years.

And I hated her and loved her for it all at once.

CHAPTER 17

IF I COULD have gone back home, I would have, but I couldn't hurt Keisha's feelings. Not after ignoring her for a week. So instead, I went with her family, walking along the River Walk to the French Quarter. Street performers entertained the crowds, and saxophone players lifted up jazz melodies over the bend in the Mississippi River. Dwayne hovered nearby, letting me push Jerome in the stroller, and Ms. Evette asked if I was all right every five minutes.

By the time we got to Café Du Monde for our beignets I would've given everything I owned to disappear. What if Loretta was right? I'd already lost my music and lied to my mother. Maybe without my singing, I *would* become disturbed.

"Hello? Earth to Tia." Keisha pulled at my sleeve, handing me a tray for my beignets.

"Huh?"

I followed her and Dwayne to the outdoor table where

Ms. Evette and Loretta sat laughing. A trumpet player set up his station outside and began to play. While everyone else ate, I closed my eyes and pictured the notes, dancing through the night sky.

"Hey, Tia." Keisha nudged me with her elbow and I had to fight my way up for air. She pointed across the street to Jackson Square. "Look. It's Kenny." We hadn't seen him since before June Fest. "Want to go talk to him?"

Loretta and Ms. Evette glanced from me to Keisha.

"Is that your boyfriend?" Loretta asked. I could just imagine what she was thinking.

Twelve years old and already she's wild.

"He's not her boyfriend . . . yet," Keisha corrected. "Can we go say hi? Please?"

Ms. Evette frowned. "I'll walk over with you," she said, but Loretta gave her the eye.

"They're old enough to cross the street on their own, Ettie," she scolded. "They don't want you hanging around while they talk to a boy. Right, girls?"

Keisha grinned. "Isn't my aunt the best?"

I didn't answer. Ms. Evette looked over at Dwayne, but he just shook his head. "Don't look at me," he said. "If I had my way, these girls wouldn't talk to a boy until they turned thirty."

Keisha rolled her eyes, then dragged me out of my chair. "Let's go."

We ran across the street, dodging the flower-covered horse-and-carriages lined up to carry tourists around the quarter. Then we wound our way through the displays of art for sale. When we'd nearly caught up to Kenny, Keisha hollered, waving like mad.

"Kenny! Hey Kenny!" She laughed at my mortified stare. "Sometimes you gotta do things quick," she whispered, "like pulling off a Band-Aid."

Kenny's family stopped a few paces ahead of us, and his mother glared, but Kenny jogged forward.

"Hi," he said, "w-what are you guys doing here?"

He was asking both of us, but looking right at me. Keisha nudged my shoulder so I'd answer.

"Getting beignets," I said, wondering how a factual statement could come out sounding so dumb.

"Oh," Kenny said. "I'm g-glad to see you."

I shuffled awkwardly. "Me too."

There was a moment of silence while Keisha pretended to study something in the distance.

"So . . . how come you weren't at June Fest?" I asked at last. "You're not quitting choir, are you?" That sounded desperate, and I wished I'd said something else.

Anything else.

Kenny smiled. "No," he said. "I was on v-v-v—" He got stuck on the sound and struggled to force it out.

"Vacation?" Keisha supplied.

"Yeah," Kenny said.

"So you'll be back?"

Kenny nodded. "On Thursday." He paused. "Why? Did you m-miss me?"

I *had* missed him. It felt so good to see him again, I wanted to burst.

"You mean at June Fest?" I blurted. "Yeah. The tenors were flat."

Keisha groaned like I was about as hopeless as they came, but Kenny didn't seem to notice.

"We're always f-flat," he said, chuckling. "Lorenzo Reyes c-can't sing on k-key to save his life."

Keisha snorted. "At least you haven't got Mary-Kate and Amber Allen trying to out-sing the whole choir. I mean, hello? It's called a choir because our voices are supposed to blend."

Showboating was one of Ms. Marion's pet peeves: *No one shines unless we all shine.*

"The choir sounds a lot better when you're there," I said to Kenny, feeling heat spread from my neck to my cheeks. But it was true. Kenny had an amazing voice—clear and steady—and when he sang he never stuttered.

"You think s-so?" Kenny asked, grinning. "M-maybe sometime w-we could—"

This time I really did wish Kenny could talk faster, because he didn't get to finish his sentence before Loretta, Ms.

Evette, Dwayne, and Jerome came up behind us. And if that wasn't bad enough, at the same time, Kenny's family came over.

Kenny's mother glared at me, as if I was already a bad influence on her son. I wondered if she knew about my father. All the adults said hello and made small talk, and the whole time I was crushed like a vise between Loretta and Kenny's mom.

I guessed Kenny had been about to ask if we could sing together, and I wanted that so bad, but right then, I wasn't sure if I'd ever sing again. What would Kenny think if he knew what my dad had done?

When I finally risked a glance in Kenny's direction, he was watching me with his head cocked to one side, studying me with warm, kind eyes.

They were the eyes of someone who knew what it felt like to be judged.

If all the adults hadn't been around, I would have reached out to hold his hand. I imagined myself squeezing lightly, the way he'd done the night of the shooting, offering up the silent truth that maybe we could do this together.

~

Since Loretta bunked with Keisha whenever she visited, Ma had swapped shifts that night, so I could sleep at home. I was relieved to be in my own bed, but I still tossed and turned, unable to sleep. I couldn't stop thinking about what Loretta had said to Ms. Evette.

One way or another, that girl is going to be disturbed.

Was that true? Did being the daughter of a murderer mean I'd grow up to do horrible things? It was as if my father had stolen my future. But really, Danielle was the one whose future had been stolen. How could I complain when at least I was still alive?

My window was open, and outside I could hear my neighbors gambling on their front porch. There was music in their voices.

Roll them bones.

Snake eyes, snake eyes.

C'mon, lady luck.

Whenever a breeze came by, the leftover Mardi Gras beads caught in the branches of the trees rattled like their dice. The sound of a calliope drifted on the wind from a riverboat far away on the Mississippi. Something about that bright, cheerful sound made me think about that other hot, humid day when I'd sung my heart out, feeling like a magician pulling scarves out of my sleeve. Then I thought about Kenny's face lighting up when he thought we might sing together.

He didn't think I was evil spawn.

But what if he was wrong?

I smacked the wall in frustration. Ma must not have been sleeping well, because in an instant, she was in my doorway, bleary-eyed with her hair sticking up in patches.

"What happened? Are you okay?"

I flopped back onto my bed. "Fine. You must have been dreaming." I wondered how come I'd never noticed how much lying Ma and I did. It was like a song on the radio that I swore I'd never heard before, but once I recognized it, I realized the DJ played it every five minutes.

"What are you still doing up?" Ma asked. "It's late."

I took a deep breath. "Ma," I said, willing myself to form the word.

Were you ever going to tell me why my father really went to prison? Did you think I'd never find out?

What I actually said surprised me. "Do you ever think about moving?"

Ma let out a little laugh and lay down onto the bed next to me. "Trust me," she said, "I've daydreamed about moving more often than you could ever guess."

I turned over, propping myself up on one elbow so we were facing each other.

"Then why don't we? We could start over someplace different. Someplace where no one knows us, and we could be anyone we want."

Ma looked at me strange. "Wouldn't you miss Keisha too much?"

The thought of missing Keisha tore through me, but I shook my head. "We'd keep in touch. Please, Ma. Let's do it."

Ma stroked my hair. "Where would we go?"

I thought it over, excitement building at the possibility that she might say yes. "California," I said. "We could live by the beach and I could audition for musicals."

Ma wrinkled her nose. "California? Really? Too crowded for me. I'd choose someplace vast and open, like Nebraska or Wyoming."

"Those would work too," I said, even though I didn't really want to live in the middle of nowhere.

Ma just sighed. "Sure would be nice if we could afford it. But you know we're lucky to have this house. If my grandmother hadn't left it to me in her will . . ." Ma closed her eyes. "Moving costs money we don't have and, frankly, I don't know where I'd be without Ms. Evette to help out with you. I know this isn't the best area, but we have to make do with what we have. You understand that, don't you, Tia?"

I stared up at the ceiling. Tears stung my eyes.

"Yeah," I said. "It's just . . . I wish . . ."

"What do you wish, honey?"

I wish I didn't live in the same city as Danielle Morton's family.

I shook my head. "Nothing. You should go back to bed. I know you have to work early tomorrow."

"That's true." Ma got up slowly. She walked over to the doorway and stopped. "You know I love you, right? If there's something bothering you, you'd tell me?"

Ma looked so concerned, standing there in her tattered

nightshirt, that I didn't have the heart to hurt her. "Nothing's wrong," I murmured, but the minute I said it, I understood something important.

Lying was exhausting.

So was hiding. I didn't want to be the person Keisha's aunt Loretta thought I'd become. I wanted to be the girl who'd dreamed of changing the world with her voice. I wanted to be the girl who could sing duets with a really great guy if he asked her to.

But now I knew that wouldn't happen unless I *made* it happen. If Ma wouldn't be leaving this city any time soon, then there was something I needed to do.

Something that made my heart pound and my throat constrict.

Something that scared me straight down to my bones.

CHAPTER 18

THE NEXT NIGHT I was back at Keisha's. We'd begged for this sleepover, since we'd missed the one on Monday night.

"Are you sure you need to do this?" Keisha asked. Her room was dark and we were hiding under the sheet, lighting the space with a tiny flashlight. "I just don't see how going to Danielle Morton's house will do anything other than make things worse."

I shook my head. "I told you already. I need to go back to where things went wrong, and if I don't apologize, no one ever will."

Keisha groaned. "But it wasn't *your* fault! You were four! How exactly were you supposed to stop your butt-brained father from using his stupid butt-brain to do something stupid?"

She was getting riled up, but I didn't care.

"It's not about whose fault it is. Now that I know what

happened, I need to tell Danielle's family that I'm sorry my father was such a stupid butt-brain!"

Despite ourselves, this made us both giggle, and moments later we heard Ms. Evette's voice holler up the stairs.

"Girls, quiet! Go to sleep!"

Keisha and I exchanged glances, listening for footsteps in the hallway, but there weren't any.

"Too bad Auntie Loretta went back to Mississippi," Keisha said at last. "She would've driven you there. I'm sure of it."

I started to agree, but then I stopped. This was as good a time as any to start telling the truth.

"Keisha," I said. "Your aunt Loretta hates me."

"What?!" Keisha demanded. "That's not true. Why would you say that?"

I took a deep breath. "I overheard her and your ma talking. Loretta thinks I'm going to turn out like my father."

Keisha's eyes widened. "But she always brings you presents when she visits. And she seems so happy to see you."

"I know," I said, "but she's just doing that for you. I know you're crazy about your aunt, and that's fine, but I don't think I'll visit next time she's here."

Keisha was quiet for a long time. "I guess that's why everyone was so tense the other night. Feels crappy that I didn't know." She paused. "I'm really sorry."

I nodded. "It's not your fault, but I bet it still feels good to apologize for it."

This time Keisha's eyes narrowed. "Fine," she said at last. "You've made your point. If you *have* to do this, I'll help. It'll have to be during choir rehearsal, though. This isn't like sneaking out my window for twenty minutes. It's gonna take you a long time to get there and a long time to get back, and it's not like you can just rush in, apologize, and then run right out again." Keisha paused, thinking things over. "How about this: I'll tell Mama that you're going to be late to choir rehearsal because . . ."

"'Cause Ma's shift changed again?"

"Good. That way Mama won't be looking for you when we get there."

"What if your mom decides to stay and watch?"

"She won't. She's got all the sheets and towels to wash from Auntie Loretta's visit, and Jerome is cutting a tooth, so he's been fussing way too much. Wearing everyone out."

"Okay," I said. "Then I can head out when Ma leaves for work."

"You'll have to take the bus," Keisha said. "Have you ever ridden the bus on your own?"

I shook my head.

Keisha took my hand and squeezed it. "It'll be fine. Just stand up front next to the driver and listen for your stop."

"Right," I said. "I can handle that."

Footsteps sounded in the hallway and we knew Ms. Evette was coming to check on us. Keisha clicked off her flashlight and we pretended to sleep, but all I could do was lie awake, my eyes wide. Could I do this?

Was I really going to apologize for murder?

~

Thursday morning I was too nervous to eat, and when I did force down a few bites, I had to run to the bathroom to throw them up again. Ma put her hand on my forehead and scowled.

"Are you sure I don't need to stay home with you? You're white as a ghost and your eyes look glassy."

Part of me wanted to say yes—to curl up with Ma on the couch and watch mindless television where no one's problems were real and even the worst stuff got solved by the end of the episode. But I shook my head. "I'm okay," I said, fear rumbling in my gut. "Probably just one of those bugs. Besides, I've got choir rehearsal."

"Mmmm." Ma glanced at her watch. It was four o'clock and Ma was on the five p.m. to midnight shift, but it took her a while to ride the streetcar to the store on Tchoupitoulas. "All right," she said. "I have to go, but call me if you need anything. Lock the door behind you when you leave. Don't talk to strangers, and follow the path I laid out for you."

"I will," I said, watching her step outside, knowing how angry she'd be if she knew what I was about to do.

Suddenly, I couldn't remember why I'd come up with this plan in the first place. I sat on our tattered sofa, kicking my legs, determined not to chicken out. I waited half an hour just to be sure Ma wouldn't return home for some forgotten item, and once the minutes had crept by, I grabbed my house key and the extra Jazzy Pass that Ma kept in case of emergency.

Then I walked out my front door.

I almost turned around when I reached the last block where I was allowed on my own. Perspiration beaded on my forehead.

Was I doing the right thing? My whole body felt tight, and I imagined I was the jack in Jerome's jack-in-the-box and that someone was cranking the handle faster and faster until I popped. I tried to remember how it had felt to loosen up enough to sing, to throw my shoulders back and relax my jaw, but those feelings belonged to a whole other life.

At the bus stop, I had to wait forever in a crowd of milling people. Part of me wished the bus would hurry up, but another part hoped it had broken down. When it finally did arrive, I stood in line, waiting my turn to press forward up the stairs. I fed my pass into the machine, messing up twice before I got it right, then looked for an empty seat up front.

There wasn't one.

The bus was packed, all kinds of bodies jostling against one another. Little by little, I got pushed backward until I was stuck between a man in a suit and a woman with a crying baby, so I couldn't see a thing. I tried hard to hear the driver call out the names of the stops, but either he didn't yell them or I couldn't hear him.

All around me, people were squished together and the bus smelled of body odor, exhaust fumes, and fast food. Somewhere the air-conditioning was clunking away, but the wall of bodies stopped the cool air from reaching me. I started to worry I'd never get to the right stop, so in a moment of panic I pushed my way off with all the other riders at Napoleon Avenue.

It felt so good to be off the bus, I wanted to kiss the ground. I stood on the corner and pulled out my street map even though Keisha had warned me about studying a map in public.

"You'll look like a tourist," she'd said, "and then some idiot might try to rob you." It was good advice, but we both knew that a person could get robbed even if they weren't a tourist.

I looked around to orient myself and then walked down Magazine Street toward Monet. When I was almost there, I saw a building on the corner called Le Bon Temps Roule. Dwayne and Ms. Evette went there sometimes on Saturday nights, and before they left Dwayne always called out, "Let the good times roll!" Then the next day they'd tell stories about late-night music and dancing that spilled onto the street. Keisha and I had always wanted to go, but now I wondered if this was where my father had done his drinking before he'd decided to rob the Morton house.

The place didn't look like much. It was an old wooden shack with a sign out front that said BAR AND SANDWICH SHOP. There was a big chalkboard on one wall with the weekly menu, and at the top someone had written *Geaux Saints!*

I went a little farther, then turned the corner and walked down Monet Street, searching out the number on each house, but nothing looked the way I'd pictured it. The houses were average. Nicer than the shotgun houses where I lived, but not too fancy. There were a few scattered trees lining the road, and a couple of the houses had cars parked out front. I squinted hard.

Why here? Had my father stumbled down the street looking for a house that appeared unoccupied? Maybe he'd seen Mr. and Mrs. Morton at Le Bon Temps Roule, so he'd assumed their house would be empty. But how would he have known who they were or where they lived? Why couldn't he have picked a house without a twelve-year-old girl asleep in her bed? He could have chosen any place, but he'd come here. Right to . . .

1032 Monet Street.

A chain-link fence surrounded the small front yard. The house was colorful, with hot pink, yellow, and blue trim around the top to match the bright blue shutters. Two wicker chairs and a small table sat on the porch. But what made my jaw drop was the music.

All around the porch were wind chimes. They came in every size, from teeny-tiny to one that was practically as big as me, and every one of them had a butterfly on it. When the wind blew, the air filled with crystalline sound.

I knew immediately that they were for her.

"Beautiful, ain't it?" said a voice behind me. "You ought to see how many we've got over at the Butterfly Foundation. These are just Louisa's favorites."

I jumped and my heart hammered so hard, I thought it might come clean out of my chest. I whirled around, then took a step backward, nearly tripping over my own feet. An old guy with light brown wrinkly skin and silver hair stood behind me. He held up his hands as if to show that he hadn't meant to startle me. The man had a craggy face, and he was wearing the kind of plaid pants old men wear.

He chuckled softly. "Sorry. Didn't mean to—"

Then he stopped.

His gaze fixed on me, and I watched the color and kindness drain from his expression as his eyes grew dark with recognition. He took a step back before reaching up with one bony finger.

"Your face. Why, you look just like—"

I didn't wait to hear my father's name.

All thoughts of apologizing disappeared, and I sprinted down the street as fast as my legs would go.

CHAPTER 19

I NEVER SAW the sky fill with clouds. I didn't notice as the breeze picked up and turned into a strong wind. I didn't even hear the first cracks of thunder. It wasn't until the clouds opened up and drenched me with a heavy downpour that I realized a storm had been brewing. It was a typical late-day summer storm, here and gone in ten minutes, but it was enough to soak me through. By the time I reached New Heaven Baptist Church, I was shivering despite the heat, and limping from a blister on the sole of my foot.

I'd lost track of the time, and I hoped I wasn't arriving when parents would still be lingering at the back of the church. The last thing I needed was for Ms. Evette to see me like this. She'd call my mother at work and then there would be an interrogation like none other.

I slipped into the building, sliding noiselessly through the heavy wooden doors, dripping a trail onto the carpet. The Rainbow Choir was singing a gentle, rocking spiritual that

Ms. Marion said was one of her favorites, and for a moment I stood still, pressed up against the back wall, watching the chorus sway. Ms. Marion's hands danced in the air as she directed them.

She'd reorganized the choir to make up for our lost members, changing some of the altos into sopranos, and I was surprised to realize we sounded good. The melody lifted like a breeze, and though my knees felt like they'd give way, the music held me up.

Then Ms. Marion stopped abruptly in order to correct the bass section's harmony. I caught Keisha's gaze and her eyebrows furrowed when she saw my dripping wet figure. Her hand raised and waved like mad, but another hand had gone up before hers.

"Yes, Kenny?" said Ms. Marion.

"Can I go to the bathroom?"

He didn't stutter at all, but the other kids snickered anyway. Ms. Marion clucked, but she motioned for him to go.

Keisha put her hand down, half raised it again, and then she looked at me and shrugged. I swiped at my wet, tangled hair, wondering what I'd say to Kenny.

He came up beside me. "Follow me."

"But I—"

"Trust me."

Kenny led me down the steps to the adult choir room.

A row of wooden lockers lined the wall, and Kenny went over to one of the lockers and pulled out a backpack.

"Here," he said, handing me a wad of black-and-white clothing. "You can w-wear this. It's my band uniform. I come straight to rehearsal from p-practice. Might be a little big for you, but it's d-d-d . . . dry."

I shivered again. The air in the basement was cool and my clothes clung to my skin. "Thanks."

The bathrooms were down a narrow hallway, and I went into the ladies' room to change. It felt strange to be alone down here with Kenny. A voice inside my head reminded me that soon I'd have to tell him why I'd showed up late for practice, limping and drenched, but I was too numb to listen. Instead, I stripped off my wet clothes, piece by piece, and replaced them with Kenny's uniform. Then I draped my things over the sink. Maybe I could use a hand dryer on them later and return the uniform when practice was over.

Kenny's shirt smelled like him: kind of spicy with a hint of mint soap. I held the sleeve up to my nose and breathed in. Then I froze as a fragment of memory came back to me. *I was a little kid, hiding under Ma's bed, clutching the shirt I'd stolen from my father's side of the closet, breathing in his clean, fresh scent.*

I'd missed my father so bad, it had hurt.

My mouth fell open.

No. That couldn't be. It was like Keisha's aunt Loretta had said: A man had to be disturbed to pull the trigger. And I'd missed him? I thought of the way that old man had looked at me. My father's face must be branded into his mind, like a nightmare he'd never wake up from. But I'd loved him?

I couldn't help the choked noise that escaped my throat.

"Are you o-okay?"

I opened the door and shook my head.

Kenny's brown eyes looked worried, his dark lashes brushing his cheeks. He motioned to the bench in the choir room, and I followed him over. "You look really upset. Do you w-want to talk about it?"

I paused, not sure if I'd be able to get the words out, but if anyone could understand that problem, it was Kenny.

"Does it have to do with the night you f-fainted?" he pressed.

My mouth struggled to form an answer, and I was grateful that Kenny didn't rush me. Grateful, and guilty for all the times I'd rushed him.

"That night," I said at last, "I was thinking about my father. I didn't know it then, but he killed a girl. Her name was Danielle, and she was our age." I paused, waiting for Kenny's reaction, wondering if he'd known.

He let his breath out in a long, slow whistle, and I knew he was steadying himself so he wouldn't stutter. "No kidding?"

I nodded.

"I'd heard your father was in jail, but . . ." He stopped. "W-when did it happen? W-was it an accident?"

Every part of me wanted to lie, but I'd come this far.

"No," I said. "He was robbing her house. I was just four years old at the time, and he got sent to prison. For life. Ma told me about the robbery, but not the murder."

"That's aw-aw-aw—" Kenny made a rasping sound, then paused. "Awful."

"Not as awful as it must have been for Danielle's family."

We were both silent for a long time, and I was glad Kenny didn't try to make me feel better. Sometimes, better didn't exist.

"Anyway," I said, once the silence got to be too much, "ever since I found out, I can't stop thinking about what it must be like to lose someone, or to be the one who gets lost. So today I went to the girl's house to apologize, only . . ." The sound caught in my throat, and I bit my lip until I tasted blood. "I couldn't do it."

Kenny reached over and took my hand the way he had the night of the shooting. "Is this why you aren't s-singing any-more? I heard w-what happened at June Fest."

I nodded.

Kenny was quiet, as if he were thinking hard. Then he leaned forward. "You're too t-tough on yourself, Tia." He paused. "If you ask me, your f-father's the one who needs to apologize. Has he ever done that?"

I shrugged. "I don't know, but I doubt it."

"W-well, maybe it's time to make s-someone else step up for a change."

Even with the stammer, Kenny's voice was firm, and suddenly I understood that there was something noble about Kenny. He fought hard every single day for something the rest of us took for granted.

"Tia," he said, "d-did you know I joined the Rainbow Choir because of you?"

I looked up, feeling a little zing of heat under my skin. "Really? Why?"

Kenny shrugged. "Your s-singing is the most amazing thing I've ever heard in my life. And I think . . ." He paused. "I think you're really p-pretty. No. Not just pretty. Beautiful."

I drew in my breath. No one had ever told me I was beautiful. I thought of my reflection in the mirror—shades of my father's face staring back at me. I looked just like him with my brown hair and high cheekbones. How could anyone think *I* was beautiful?

"Did that sound d-d-d . . . dumb?" Kenny asked.

"No," I said. "It sounded—"

I wanted to say perfect, but I never got to finish because that's when Michael Slater came to find Kenny. He stood on the staircase peering down at us.

"Ms. Marion sent me. What's taking you so long, dude?"

We both jumped, and Michael's eyes lit up when he saw

me wearing Kenny's uniform. He hooted, pointing at Kenny. "You dog! Down here makin' out with your girlfriend?"

Kenny stood, and we both tried talking at once, but Kenny couldn't get a single word out, so Michael held up one hand. "Chill," he said. "I won't be telling nobody. But you better hurry up before Ms. Marion comes down here herself."

Kenny nodded. Then he turned to me. "You should visit your f-father," he said. "He owes you. He's the one who ought to ap-ap... apologize." He said each word slowly and carefully, and then he leaned in and kissed my cheek before bounding up the stairs and out of sight.

CHAPTER 20

THAT NIGHT Keisha and I managed to finagle another sleepover even though it meant calling my mother at work, which I was only supposed to do in emergencies. Now we sat on the fire escape in the glow of the streetlights, talking about my failed attempt to visit Danielle's family. And Kenny.

Mostly Kenny. Wasn't much to say about me wimping out.

"Man, that kid is so in love with you," Keisha said. "Imagine a boy joining a choir just to be with you. Even if it is c-c-crazy Kenny."

"Yeah," I said, distracted. My mind still buzzed with all the things Kenny had said. "Do you think I should visit my dad?" I asked aloud. "I mean, what if—"

Keisha cut me off. "No freakin' way! Your father doesn't deserve a visit from anyone, least of all you. Besides, how would you get to the prison and back without telling your mother?"

I hadn't thought about that.

"And what the heck would you say to him?"

"I don't know," I said. "I guess I'd ask him why he did it and if he's sorry."

Now that I'd said the words out loud, I thought about how good it might feel to hear my father say he was sorry. Maybe Kenny was right.

Keisha got up and ducked through her window into her bedroom. She grabbed her laptop, then came back out to sit beside me on the staircase. She typed *Louisiana State Penitentiary* into a search engine, and we both fell silent as the web page came up with a photo of the prison. I had only the one memory of visiting my father, but now the details came back—how big the place had been, and how it had looked like a fortress. There were barbed-wire fences all around, and lots of buildings shaped like X's. It was strange to look at them and think that somewhere inside, right this very minute, my father was living his life.

Keisha went to the section that said *Visitor Information* and scrolled down.

"Yup," she said, as if she'd known it all along. "Minors have to be accompanied by an adult. Plus, the adult's name has to be on the inmate's approved list of visitors."

"What about your mom?" I asked. "You think she'd be on my father's approved list?"

Keisha's mouth fell open. "Are you insane? Besides, she'd never take you there without asking your mother first."

I knew Keisha was right.

"So, I guess I should scratch that idea off the list."

"Good," Keisha said, shutting the laptop and setting it behind us. "And if you were smart, you'd stop doing depressing things and start doing fun ones. Like making out with Kenny. Trust me, that will feel *way* better than visiting your father."

I laughed. "As if you'd know anything about making out," I teased, kicking her lightly, but she got a funny look on her face.

My brows dipped into a V.

"No offense," Keisha said, shrugging, "but you're out of the loop. We've made out before rehearsal. Twice."

I gasped. "With people around? Are you crazy?" My voice shot up an octave and Keisha slapped her hand over my mouth.

"Quiet before Mama hears you. We were in the adult choir room, so no one saw us."

My cheeks burned. "What was it like?"

"Nice." Keisha grinned.

"Wow," I breathed. I couldn't believe Keisha had leapfrogged ahead of me. I tried to imagine what it might feel like to make out with Kenny, but I couldn't quite do it. I shivered.

Keisha noticed and laughed. "You're thinking about Kenny, aren't you?"

I blushed and Keisha grinned. "Just wait. We're gonna get all this stuff figured out and then next time we travel for a concert, me and Khalil and you and Kenny can steal the back seats of the bus, and canoodle the whole way. Then we'll sing so loud that everyone in New Orleans will hear about the Rainbow Choir, and we'll never be short of members again. Amen."

Me and Keisha leaned back against the stairs, and I looked up into the branches of the magnolia tree high above us, trying to imagine God sitting among the stars listening to Keisha's wish turned prayer and deciding whether or not we were worthy of making out with boys in the backseat of a bus.

Then I thought about Ma, sitting on the steps of her high school, smiling up at her boyfriend like he hung the moon. Was that how Keisha looked at Khalil? Made the hairs on my arms stand up straight, so I decided to change Keisha's prayer. *God,* I prayed, *forget about the bus. Just don't bring Keisha any trouble.*

CHAPTER 21

THE NEXT MORNING, we were listening to music in Keisha's room. It was raining outside and every now and then a rumble of thunder sounded in the distance. We'd cracked Keisha's window just enough to let in a little bit of cool air, and it smelled like mud puddles with an occasional whiff of magnolia.

I was on YouTube looking for silly videos, and Keisha was sprawled on her bed, texting Khalil fast and furious.

"Oooh," Keisha said. "He's lovin' me."

She typed something back, and then giggled as another text message chimed.

"He says I'm the best-looking girl in New Orleans, but I'm typing, 'Only New Orleans?'"

A minute later she grinned. "Okay. Now he says the whole world." She turned to me. "Think I should say I want to be Miss Universe? Or wait, maybe I can tell him he's Mr. Universe to me."

Keisha and I both groaned at how corny that sounded.

"Lame," I said. "Try something else."

Keisha nibbled at the plastic casing of her phone. "I've got it," she said after a minute had passed. But before she could type anything, her phone chimed again.

"Silly boy," she muttered. "I can't even keep up." Then she paused, frowning slightly. "He says he wants to meet me tonight. We've never gotten together outside of choir before." She shrugged. "Guess you can't blame him for wanting something extra."

"Tell him he'll have to wait," I said, typing the words *singing cats*. "It's pouring outside."

Keisha frowned. "He's telling me he wants to kiss me," she said, but she didn't sound happy this time. She sounded confused, and that made my stomach twist into a knot. Keisha's eyes narrowed. "He says I promised we'd meet at the library uptown if he took the streetcar."

"Did you say that?"

"Of course not! Why the heck would I want to meet uptown?"

"So if he's not replying to you, then . . ."

Keisha's jaw fell open as another text message chimed in. "Mary-Kate?" she read aloud. Keisha's eyes shot open and she hurled her phone across the room. If it didn't have the shatter-proof case, it would have broken for sure. "He's fooling around with Mary-Kate?" she repeated. "How . . .

since when?" She was sputtering, her cheeks flushed with rage.

A message chimed, and then a minute later her phone rang, but neither of us moved to answer it.

"That jerk!" I breathed. Even though I wasn't the one who'd gotten cheated on, my heart still raced. "How could he do that?"

"So, this whole time he's been texting me," Keisha said, as if she was still trying to piece things together, "he's also been texting Mary-Kate?" Her breathing was ragged and her fists clenched. "But she's so stuck-up! Why would he want to fool around with her?"

The phone had stopped ringing, but now it started again, making us both jump. Keisha shook her head numbly. "I let that boy touch me," she whispered, "like he had some right to, and now . . . Do you think I'm not a good enough kisser?"

I got up and sat beside Keisha on the bed, putting my arm around her shoulders. "It's not your fault," I said. "Mary-Kate probably stole him away on purpose just to be mean. You know she hates us both. If he fell for her act, he's a loser."

Keisha threw herself down on the bed and buried her face in her pillow.

"I'm the loser," she said, her voice muffled. "Why did I ever trust him? I let him talk me into—"

She didn't finish her sentence, and I wondered if Keisha had done more than she was telling me. But this wasn't the time to ask, so I rubbed her back instead. "You couldn't have known. He seemed so cool, and I swear he liked you."

Keisha sobbed, and a minute later, her bedroom door opened and Ms. Evette stepped inside. She had Jerome with her, and she set him down on the floor beside me.

"This is about that boy," Ms. Evette said, like it wasn't even a question. I moved over so she could scoop Keisha up.

"Now you listen to me," she said. "Both of you. There are a lot of boys out there who will do you wrong, but there are also a lot of them who will do right by you. Most of the time you'll know the difference, but if you make a mistake, you've got to know in your heart that he's the fool who's losing out."

Keisha only cried harder, so Ms. Evette took her by the shoulders.

"You are my beautiful daughter, and the boy you end up with will be blessed to have you. So this little . . . twerp . . . who's passed you up, or done whatever stupid thing he's done, well, he just missed out on being the luckiest boy alive."

This made Keisha sniff a tiny bit, and then Jerome crawled over and put his finger up her nose.

"Jerome!" she sputtered.

Keisha's phone chimed again and Ms. Evette picked it up. She looked like she wanted to hurl it too, but she just turned it off.

"I came up to tell you that Tia's mother would like her to come home."

There was something in her tone that shot a ripple of fear down my spine. "Is everything okay?" I asked.

Ms. Evette paused. "Your mama didn't sound too happy, hon."

Keisha and I stared at each other, our eyes saying all the things our mouths couldn't. Finally, I whispered one tiny plea.

"But I can't leave Keisha."

Ms. Evette patted my shoulder. "I'll take care of Keisha," she said, nodding toward the door. "Dwayne's waiting to walk you home."

I guessed Ms. Evette knew more than she was telling. I also guessed that Ma calling me home early so soon after I'd visited Danielle Morton's house was more than a coincidence.

Somehow, my mother knew.

CHAPTER 22

WHEN I GOT home, Ma was waiting in the kitchen, her body rigid. Dwayne walked me inside, shaking out his huge orange-and-black umbrella, and then he squeezed my shoulder. "I know this is a difficult time for you," he said, "but just remember that things will work out in the long run. They always do."

I wanted to believe that, but I knew bad stuff didn't go away simply because time passed. Sometimes it got worse.

The moment Dwayne left, my mother pointed to a chair. "Sit," she commanded. I took the high-backed wooden chair at the kitchen table, my hands trembling. Outside, a siren wailed and another clap of thunder made the thin walls of our house shake.

"*How could you*?" Ma rumbled.

Nothing echoes like those words. I didn't say anything, unsure of what she knew.

"He came by the store today," Ma said. A sob choked in

her throat and she put the back of her wrist up to her mouth to stop it. "That little girl's grandfather came to the Winn-Dixie and asked for me because apparently my daughter—"

She stopped, struggling to speak through her fury. "Because my daughter paid them a visit," Ma hissed. She said the words as if she thought it was as bad as breaking into the Mortons' house like my father had all those years before.

"How could you *do* such a thing?" Ma demanded. "Do you think our family hasn't done them enough harm?"

"*You* never told me the truth!" I yelled.

"Told you the truth? Everything I've done has been to allow you to *forget*! And now the first thing you do after you find out is to march over to the Mortons' house? What were you thinking? How long have you known?"

"Long enough," I snapped. "But I didn't go to Danielle's house to hurt anyone."

Ma flinched when I said Danielle's name. "What was it, then?" she spat. "Curiosity? Fascination?" Her words dripped with shame.

"You certainly weren't thinking about the Mortons, but did you give a single thought to me? Do you have any idea what it was like for me to see that man again? I can't imagine how he knew where I worked, but there he was all tender and concerned like I've lost control of yet another one of my—"

This time the sob came out loud and full, and it seemed

to take even Ma by surprise. Her shoulders shook and she fell to her knees on the kitchen floor. It wasn't pretty crying. Her mouth hung open for a second before she could contain the wail, and then she just stayed there, rocking back and forth as the rain beat against the kitchen window. A trickle of water forced its way through a crack in the seal and streamed down the wall and onto the linoleum.

I got up and walked over to Ma, not sure whether I should try to comfort her or not. Gingerly, I reached my arms around her, but she pushed me away. Hard. I stumbled backward, feeling as if my house of cards was finally falling over.

"Ma," I pleaded when her sobs had slowed down. *"Please."*

I wasn't even sure what I was asking for, but Ma shook her head.

"You have no idea, Tia," she said. "You don't have any idea what it was like, and all I want is to put this whole thing behind us, but apparently that's too much to ask. Your father broke my heart, and he sure as hell broke their hearts, and now you go dredging everything up after all this time. Why? Why would you do that?"

The trickle of water was turning into a stream, spreading across the kitchen floor, but I didn't move. Ma stood up and leaned against the refrigerator as the water trailed between us.

"I didn't mean to," I whispered at last. "I wasn't trying to hurt anyone. It's just that you never talked about what happened, and I have so many questions."

Ma's face was hard. "Don't make excuses."

"I'm not," I sputtered. "I just wanted answers and I didn't think—"

"You're darn right you didn't think," Ma interrupted. "You were just being a *sightseer.*" She said that word like it was the worst word that had ever been invented. "Do you have any idea how many sightseers came around after your father went to prison? People came by to sneer, to spit on our porch steps, to smash the car window . . . All of those judging eyes: my coworkers at the store, folks at church, people on the street when I was walking you to school. Do you really think you would've had a better life if I'd told you what your father did?"

I shivered uncontrollably. "Maybe if I'd known all along . . ."

"What good would that have done?" Ma snapped. "I've given up everything to keep this mess away from you. You think I wouldn't like to go out and do things like any normal person? But the last thing you need is me there, reminding everyone what happened."

I stared in disbelief.

"Is that why you never go to my concerts? Or June Fest? Or school functions?"

"Somebody has to protect you!"

I took a step toward Ma.

"You call that protecting me?" I hollered. "Maybe if you'd gone and let people stare, they would've gotten over it eight years ago and I could have had at least one of my parents around."

That's when Ma slapped me. Her hand shot out so quick, I never saw it coming. Thunder crashed again, as if the outside world was trying to cover up what Ma had just done, one sound canceling out the other, but the falsetto pitch of the slap was louder than the bass of the thunder.

I froze.

Ma half lifted her hand as if she might try to smooth away the sting, but then she put it down again. A gust of wind smacked sheets of rain against the window, and I had a crazy urge to grab the cast-iron pan from the stove and smash the glass, letting all the wind and rain howl inside.

Ma's face flushed a deep pink.

"You want to know everything?" she said at last, her chest heaving. "Fine. Your father shot a girl and came home with blood on his hands. It dripped on the floor right where you're standing, and when he told me what he'd done, I screamed so loud, you hid in the closet behind the brooms and dust mop, and I couldn't get you to come out for the rest of the night. And you know what I did, Tia? I got on my hands and knees and scrubbed that girl's blood off the floor. Took me days."

I should have been shocked, but as soon as the words were out of my mother's mouth, I remembered. The memories blossomed like the blood that had dripped off my father's wrist.

He'd brought home the gun, wanting Ma to get rid of it, and they'd fought about whether or not she should help him because that would make her an accomplice, and if she went to prison, who would be left to take care of me?

I remembered the sounds of their voices. The sweaty, filthy smell of my father. My mother's hysterical scream. The cloying heat of the closet, and the slam of the front door when my father finally left.

The memories were all there, exactly where they had always been.

Locked inside.

I stumbled to the table and sat down hard on a kitchen chair. I waited for the tears, but they didn't come. Leaking rainwater swirled around me, but I felt parched and dry as a bone. Finally, Ma came over, and this time she really did reach out to stroke my cheek, right where it stung from the slap.

"I'm sorry, Tia," she said at last. "I'm so, so sorry. For everything."

She put her arms around me, and for a long time we simply held each other tight, listening to the rain. I thought I might never speak again, but eventually I forced a single word from my throat.

"Why?"

Ma seemed to understand what I meant.

"I don't know," Ma whispered back. "I don't think your father even knows."

We sat there in silence again, exhaustion overtaking us both. Ma shook her head. "I swore I'd never raise a hand to you," she said. "I wish I could take it back."

As if life gave do-overs.

We both knew better.

I curled my feet under me, trying to warm them up. "The old man," I said at last, "was he angry? Did he hate me for going over there?"

Ma sighed. "No," she said at last. "He said he was sorry that he scared you." She shook her head. "I've never apologized to them. Once I sent an anonymous card that said I was sorry for their loss, but I didn't think they'd want to hear from me, and in the courtroom things were always so . . . tense.

"I should have been the one to say I was sorry, and instead there he was all these years later apologizing to *me* at the counter of the Winn-Dixie." Her chin dropped. "Oh, Tia. I'm such a coward."

She reached into her pocket and took out a piece of yellow paper that had been crumpled into a ball. "Mr. Morton asked me to give you this," she said. "I was so angry, I wasn't going to tell you, but you deserve to know." She paused. "He said he heard the Rainbow Choir sing at June Fest, and he wondered if you might participate in their fund-raiser. He's especially interested in you singing the lead."

She handed me the paper and ever so slowly, I unfolded the creases and smoothed it out against my leg. It was a flyer, and all around the edges were butterflies.

The Butterfly Foundation
invites you to
our annual fund-raiser at
Audubon Park
to benefit families who have been
the victims of violence
August 4
12:00 to 4:00 P.M.
Food, entertainment, and fun!

I took a deep, shuddering breath, remembering the angry stares at June Fest. Someone from the Morton family had been there and I hadn't even known it? I tried to remember if I'd seen butterflies on any of the posters around the courtyard, but I couldn't recall. Why would Mr. Morton ask me to sing the lead when he'd seen me fail so spectacularly that night?

I shook my head. Maybe I'd tell Ms. Marion about the invitation, but even if the Rainbow Choir sang, I didn't plan on showing up. It was too much to ask.

I understood why my mother had crumpled up the paper. How could we possibly go to a fund-raiser organized by Danielle's family?

But another question lingered behind that one.

How could they have invited us?

CHAPTER 23

On Saturday I went over to Keisha's place and found her on the couch watching TV in her pajamas. Her hair was sticking up, and she was watching reruns on the Cartoon Network. The TV blared, and she wouldn't turn it off even when I suggested we go up to her room and listen to music instead.

"Nah," she said. "I'm watching this."

"*SpongeBob* reruns?"

"Yeah."

She was crunching on Doritos even though it was only ten a.m.

"Did you talk to Khalil?" I asked.

"Yup," she said, popping the *p* sound. "I broke up with him, of course, and he said he was sorry and it was all Mary-Kate's fault, and he'd never do it again. Blah, blah, blah." She rolled her eyes. "Can't trust fools like him. They say what you want to hear, and if you're stupid enough to believe it, they'll suck you right back in. But I'm not gonna be a fool twice."

I plopped down on the couch beside her.

"That's good, right?"

"Uh-huh," Keisha said, but she sounded hard. Then she softened a little. "What happened with your mama? Was it bad?"

"Beyond bad," I said. "Bad doesn't even begin to cover it. We had the hugest fight ever. Ma cried. And she slapped me."

"She did what?!"

I nodded. "Told you it was bad. But the good news is, we finally talked about my father. She told me what happened after . . . you know . . . afterward. There was stuff I hadn't remembered until she said it—horrible stuff like my dad bringing home the gun and Ma screaming when she heard what he'd done—but I'm glad I finally have my memories back."

"Why would you *want* to remember stuff like that?" Keisha asked.

I shrugged. "I guess it's like you said when you first told me about my father being a murderer. It's better to know the truth."

Keisha frowned. "I'm not so sure I feel that way anymore. Sometimes the truth sucks."

"Yeah," I agreed. "But without it . . . I've decided I'm going to ask Ma about visiting my dad."

Keisha sat up. "You're gonna do *what*?!" I couldn't believe the fire in her eyes. "I thought we decided you wouldn't do that, and now you're telling me you're going to see that . . . that . . ."

She was searching for just the right hateful word.

"He's my father," I argued. "I thought you'd agree that I can't hide like my mom. If she says she'll take me to the prison, then I want to go."

"Making a smart decision isn't the same thing as hiding," Keisha said, enunciating the words. "Your father is a user and a liar, and you're giving him a signed invitation to walk all over your heart. You think he's not going to talk and talk, trying to get you to see him more often? Do you truly believe he's not going to say everything you ever wanted to hear? Why would you even think you could trust that man?"

She stood up and stormed out of the living room, and I was left sitting on the sofa with my mouth hanging open. Dwayne came in carrying Jerome and sat down on the opposite end of the couch, whistling softly through his teeth.

"Hoo-boy, we men are bad news," he said. "Bad, bad, bad." He bounced Jerome on one knee. "You bad news, son? 'Cause I think you're trouble just waiting to happen." Jerome was wearing a green onesie and a hat with puppy dog ears. Dwayne turned to me. "He looks like trouble, doesn't he? I mean, look at those big, brown deceivin' eyes. Look at this bad-boy getup."

"Da," Jerome said, and Dwayne's eyebrows shot up.

"You hear that? What kind of lies are you spewing?"

Jerome grinned a great big drooly smile, and I laughed despite everything.

Dwayne laughed too, and then he looked at me. "Don't mind Keisha. She's a bit worked up right now, but she'll get over it. Did I hear you say you're going to ask about visiting your father?"

I nodded and Dwayne thought it over.

"I'm not going to lie," he said. "You can't watch a woman cry the way your mama cried and not hate the source of those tears just a tiny bit. I used to watch you and Keisha so Evette could sit with your mother at the courthouse, and you got real quiet during those months. You bounced back, but never to the same point you'd started. I remember when you and Keisha were both these squirming, laughing, screaming, running-around, singing, dancing little girls with hardly a care in the world, and then . . ."

Dwayne sighed.

"I became disturbed?"

"No," Dwayne said, poking me hard. "Loretta . . . she doesn't know all that she thinks she knows. There will always be people who want to judge, but no one knows what will come out of adversity. It's different for every single person. Some people turn hard, and others, well . . . Want to know what came out for you?"

I nodded.

"Your voice. After your father went to prison, you started

to sing like Mahalia, something deep and powerful flowing out of that tiny body. First time I heard you sing like that, I was looking around the house to see where the stereo had gotten moved to." He laughed. "Then I came around a corner and there you were. Nearly knocked me off my feet."

"I thought I'd always been able to sing," I said, but Dwayne wagged his finger.

"Oh, you could always *sing,*" he said, "but before your daddy went to prison, you sang the notes, and afterward you sang with heart. Anyway," Dwayne said, "for what it's worth, I think you're doing the right thing."

Dwayne poked me in my sternum. "You're strong, Tia. Right here at your core." He glanced up the stairs. "My princess is strong too; she just doesn't remember it right now. But she will."

I got up and hugged Dwayne tight, scooping Jerome into the embrace. "Thanks."

Dwayne grinned. "Don't mention it. We men have our moments, don't we? I mean, most of the time we're just full-on rotten." He made a mean face. "We're bad, bad Leroy Browns. Baddest men in the whole dang town."

"Da," Jerome said.

I smiled, feeling the shadow of a song creeping in, right where Dwayne had poked me.

~

I went home and for the rest of the day I tried to do normal things, but all I could think about was Keisha. Didn't feel right for us to fight. Not after all that had happened.

That night I called her cell phone.

"Hello?"

"Keisha?"

"Uh-huh."

"It's me. Tia."

Keisha sighed. "Duh. You think I don't know your voice?" She was short and snappy, as if I'd annoyed her.

"I wanted to know if we could talk."

Keisha was quiet.

"Listen," I said. "I get that my father probably doesn't deserve anything—not even a visit—but he's the only father I've got."

"Just tell me one thing," Keisha said at last. "If you visit your father, are you planning on forgiving him? For murder? For leaving you and your mama alone? Could you really let him off the hook for all that?"

Now it was my turn to be silent.

"Well?" Keisha prompted.

"I don't know," I said. "Maybe deep down, I *do* want to forgive him. If he's sorry, I mean."

There. I'd made my confession.

Keisha exploded. "*What?!* After what he did to that little girl and her family . . . Honestly, Tia, he's a sick, twisted *murderer.* How could you even sit in the same room with him? You're so much better off without him, and if you forgive him, it's like saying that what he did was okay. Would you forgive the men who killed that baby?"

I wanted to defend my father—say that this was an entirely different situation—but I couldn't because that wasn't true. I thought about the Raven woman. What would she think if she knew I wanted to visit my father in jail?

"I didn't say I *would* forgive him," I said at last. "I just want to talk."

"And you don't think he'll convince you to come back for more visits? To have some kind of relationship with him?"

"Would that be so horrible?" I said. "He probably doesn't even want to see me, but if he does . . . if my own father remembers I exist . . ." I paused. "If you weren't so angry about Khalil, you'd understand."

"Leave Khalil out of this," Keisha spat. "He hasn't got anything to do with your stupid butt-brained father."

This time those words didn't sound funny at all.

"Keisha," I sputtered. "You're being selfish. You get a hundred hugs a week from your dad and you take them all for granted. You've been treated right for twelve years and now because of this one guy—"

"Don't even go there!" Keisha shouted. "You think *I'm* being selfish? Then how come your mother was on the phone with my mom last night, crying for hours? 'Cause you sure haven't been thinking of her. As for Khalil . . . at least the guy I fooled around with was hot, unlike Kenny, who's a total nerd. At least I've kissed *some*one."

Keisha was hitting below the belt, and she knew it. But I could hit below the belt too. "Yeah?" I said. "And you've done a whole lot more than that, so how's it working out for you?"

We both went silent.

I opened my mouth to apologize, but Keisha sniffed loudly on the other end. "A best friend would never say that," she said.

"A best friend wouldn't judge me for wanting to visit my father."

"Fine," Keisha said. "Then maybe we're not best friends anymore."

"Maybe we're not."

Keisha snorted. "Hope you and your dad enjoy each other."

Then the phone went dead with a final click.

CHAPTER 24

THE LAST THING I wanted was to see Keisha again so soon after our fight, but the next night was Monday, so I didn't have a choice. I went over to Keisha's place as usual, but there was nothing usual about the visit. Keisha stayed in her room all afternoon while I sat in front of the television. The whole time, Ms. Evette made disapproving noises under her breath.

When dinner rolled around, Keisha and I sat at opposite ends of the table.

"Could I have the salt please?" I asked, a little too gruffly.

The salt was next to Keisha's plate, but she didn't move to pass it. Dwayne raised an eyebrow.

"What?" Keisha said. "She was asking you, not me."

"Watch that tone," Dwayne warned. He and Ms. Evette shared an exasperated look, and Keisha glared as if it were my fault she'd gotten scolded. She slid the salt across the table, then waited a minute before fixing me with a stare.

"Well? Aren't you going to pass it back?"

"You didn't ask for it," I snapped. "How was I supposed to know you wanted salt?"

"Because it was sitting by my plate!"

"Then you should have used it before you passed it to me."

"Maybe you should have thought to ask if I was done with it!"

"Why do I always have to be the thoughtful one?"

"Why do I always have to help you out?"

"I don't need you to do anything for me!"

"Well, I don't need *you* either because—"

That's when Ms. Evette blew through her teeth in the loudest, shrillest whistle I'd ever heard. "Enough!"

Jerome started to cry and Dwayne made a face that said we were in for it now. Ms. Evette stood up, took both of our full plates away, and put them on the kitchen counter.

"The two of you," she said slowly, "are going upstairs to Keisha's bedroom to work this out. If you succeed before bedtime, you may come down and finish your dinners. If not, these plates can be your breakfasts, your lunches, or tomorrow's dinners. I don't care if they grow green mold on them. Now go."

Keisha and I glared at each other and neither of us moved, but then Dwayne cleared his throat. "You heard the queen," he said. "Go on."

Keisha ran up the stairs, but I took my time. When I

reached her room the door was shut, but since I didn't have anyplace else to go, I opened it and went in. Keisha was lying facedown on her bed, taking up the entire space. I sat at her desk and turned on the laptop, staring at the screen.

Half an hour passed. Then forty-five minutes.

Ms. Evette came upstairs and stuck her head inside the door. She looked from me to Keisha. "Okay," she said. "Your dinners are getting cold and slimy. And yes, you will be eating your collard greens no matter what time of day I serve your meals." The door shut loudly behind her.

Keisha balled up her fist and smacked the bed.

Half an hour after that, Dwayne snuck the door open and sent Jerome crawling inside. He kept making little gurgly sounds, and then he pulled himself up so he could walk while holding on to the side of the bed. He grinned because he was so proud of his big accomplishment. No matter how mean and ugly I wanted to be, it's nearly impossible to be mad when a baby is around.

I smiled at the same time as Keisha, but then we both stopped. Keisha picked up Jerome and handed him back out to Dwayne.

"Leave us alone, Dad."

Dwayne said, "Huh? What? Oh, did Jerome get in there? What a sneaky little guy." He swooped Jerome up. "Were you in there being cute? Darn you! Enough with the innocent act.

You get away from me again and . . ." Dwayne placed Jerome back inside the room, and Jerome waved his arms while making a raspberry.

I stifled a smile as Keisha picked him up, saying, "I told you—"

"It's not me," Dwayne said, throwing both hands in the air. "It's him. Holler at your baby brother."

Keisha plopped Jerome into Dwayne's arms and then she tried to push Dwayne down the hall. "Go away!"

Dwayne dug in his heels so Keisha had to stand there with her hands on his back and her feet slipping on the carpet, like a cartoon character. Dwayne just laughed before hopping away quick so Keisha went sprawling. Jerome giggled and pointed.

"You're rotten," Keisha shouted. "That was so mean."

"Baddest boys in the whole dang town," Dwayne sang, walking down the hall with Jerome.

Keisha got up and brushed off her shorts, and then she came back in and shut the door, shaking her head. "I swear. Can't a girl be mad around here?"

"Yeah," I agreed. "This is our first real fight and they won't even let us have it in peace."

Keisha's face broke into a tiny, fleeting smile. "Do you even remember what we were fighting about?"

I shrugged. "I think it was because you made a mistake

with Khalil and I threw it in your face, which was pretty awful, considering how many mistakes I've made and you've never done that."

Keisha sat down on the floor and leaned against her bed. "Nah," she said at last. "I think it was because you want to visit your dad and instead of being supportive, I judged you for it."

I sighed. "I understand why you hate my father. Most of me hates him too. But this other little part wishes none of this had ever happened, so he could have just been my dad. You know?"

"Sort of," Keisha said. She paused. "Tia? Will you promise not to get mad if I tell you something?"

"I guess."

Keisha glanced at me sideways. "When I found out what your father did," Keisha said, "I thought your mother was really weak. I kept wondering why she got together with him in the first place, and how come she didn't stop him, as if she should have seen the murder coming. Plus, I've always thought she was wrong for not going out and doing stuff with you."

Keisha shook her head.

"But now I'm sorry I judged her, 'cause I didn't see trouble coming with Khalil, and everyone in choir has been texting about it, laughing at how stupid I was not to see that he was playing me. And that whole time I just thought he was perfect. Guess I don't want the same thing to happen to you."

"Keisha," I said, "first of all, I couldn't tell about Khalil either. And second of all, I *know* my dad isn't perfect."

Keisha frowned. "Yeah. But I guess what I'm trying to say is . . . I can understand why your mom tried so hard to protect you."

I wasn't sure what to say, but before I could answer, Keisha sighed. "You know," she said, "I always assumed I'd be like my mother. I'd be the strong one who would make all the right decisions. And I'd have the fabulous love story. But instead . . ." She looked at me, her eyes watering, and for the first time I could see what I'd been missing all along.

"Are you telling me you're jealous? *Of me?*"

My face must have showed pure shock, because Keisha laughed. "Tia, no one else can sing like you can. You've got this amazing talent. I know we both pretend we're going to be stars, but you're the only one who might actually succeed. And then on top of that, a really nice guy is head-over-heels in love with you."

"Wow," I breathed. "But you're so much prettier than me, and you make friends a lot easier, and you have the best family ever."

Keisha smiled. "Can't argue with the last part," she said, "even if they do drive me crazy sometimes. But you're prettier than you think."

She nudged me with her foot, and I couldn't help smiling.

"Keisha?" I said.

"Uh-huh?"

"I have something to show you." I'd been carrying the square of yellow paper with the fund-raiser invitation in my pocket ever since Ma gave it to me, and now I took it out and unfolded it on the floor between us. "They want the Rainbow Choir to perform 'I know,' and they asked me to sing the lead."

Keisha's mouth fell open. "They what?" She shook her head as if she couldn't quite believe what I was telling her. "No offense, but why would they do that?"

I'd been wondering the same thing. "Honestly?" I said. "I have no idea."

"Whoa," Keisha breathed. "That's huge." For a moment she was stunned into silence, but then she looked up at me. "So when are you going to tell Ms. Marion? Don't you dare let Mary-Kate sing the lead. And I'm not even saying that because of Khalil. You sing it so much better than she does."

Keisha was moving ahead as if the decision had already been made, but my throat felt dry and my pulse pounded in my temples.

"Keisha," I said, "I couldn't sing a note at June Fest, and I didn't even know Danielle's family was there that night. If I choked at the fund-raiser, it would be so much worse. I'm not sure I have the guts to show up, let alone sing."

Keisha's brow wrinkled. "Of course you can do it," she said, reaching over to stroke my arm. "This will be different from June Fest because they've invited you. Just imagine . . .

we joined the Rainbow Choir so we could make a difference, and now we'll be able to help raise money for a great cause. And we can use our voices to make people stop and think. Isn't that what you've always wanted?"

I couldn't argue with that. It *was* what I'd always hoped would happen. And there was no doubt that Lyle Frank's daughter singing at Danielle Morton's fund-raiser would make people think. But what if all they thought was that I shouldn't be there?

I remembered the woman yanking the soap out of my hand at June Fest, and heard Mary-Kate's harsh whisper. *I can't believe you showed up. That's nervy. Considering.*

But then I thought about standing in front of the baby's house, and knowing I had the perfect song to sing. What if my voice was the one gift I could truly offer ?

CHAPTER 25

THE NEXT DAY, I decided to talk to Ma. I should have had my lesson with Ms. Marion that morning, but since we were still on break, I didn't have any excuse to put things off.

When I got home from Keisha's, Ma was standing in an ocean of bubble wrap. I stood in the middle of the kitchen and cleared my throat. "Ma," I said, determined to force the words out, "can we talk?"

Ma sighed. "Haven't we done enough of that lately?"

Wasn't exactly the start I'd been hoping for.

"It's just . . . I've been thinking about that invitation. To the fund-raiser."

"And?"

"And . . ." *I want to say yes.* "It's exactly the type of thing Ms. Marion would want us to do, so it would be wrong to keep this from her. Don't you think?"

I could see the wariness in Ma's entire body. She'd been

packaging several small porcelain figurines, but now she set them down.

“Are you saying . . . I mean . . . would you want to sing too?”

I shrugged. “I’ve been thinking about it. Keisha thinks I should.” I paused. “What do you think?”

Ma sat down at the kitchen table. Sagged was more like it. She held her head in her hands and rubbed her temples. I could practically see the migraine coming on, and guilt spread from my head to my toes.

“I know your singing is important to you, Tia,” she said at last, “and you have real talent. But this . . .”

My chest constricted and for a moment I couldn’t breathe. My body felt hot and sweaty, and my skin prickled. *She was going to say no.*

“Ma,” I blurted, “why didn’t you deliver the bread?”

Ma looked up like this was the last thing she’d expected.

“Don’t lie again,” I said. “I stopped by the house to write a note, so I know it wasn’t there. Do you think we’re not good enough to do anything nice? Is it because we’re bad people?”

Ma reached out and grabbed my hand, pulling me toward her.

“No,” she said. “That’s . . . good Lord, Tia. How could you think such a thing? Of course you’re good enough. Your choir is wonderful. You’re wonderful!”

"How would you know?" I spat. "You've never come to a concert or to any of our rehearsals."

Now Ma's cheeks flushed, and her nostrils flared as she drew in her breath. I waited for her anger. Maybe she'd slap me again. But this time she only nodded.

"You're right."

My jaw fell open, and I had to force it shut.

"I am?"

"Of course you are. And you're right about the bread too. I should have delivered it. I don't know why I didn't, except... I was scared." She ran her fingers through her hair. "I know it's hard for you to understand, but I think I've been scared for the last eight years." Ma searched my eyes. "Sometimes when something terrible happens—something you never saw coming—you live the rest of your days protecting yourself from the next terrible thing."

I thought that over.

"Ma?" I asked. "Did you ever ask Dad why he murdered Danielle? I mean, what he did changed everything. For everybody. Don't you want to know why?"

Ma's eyes filled with tears and she shook her head. "I don't think there's an answer to that question."

"What if I wanted to ask anyway?"

The silence between us stretched on a long time, but finally Ma cleared her throat, her voice cracking. "Are you asking to visit your father in prison?"

I bit my lip. "I've been thinking about it."

Ma got up and paced the length of the kitchen. Then she sat down at the table and traced the grooves in the wood with her nail, etching deeper and deeper.

"Is this why you've stopped singing?" Ma asked at last.

I looked up, and Ma sighed.

"I don't miss half as much as you think I do. I might have missed the fact that you'd find out about the murder on your own and then go over to the Mortons' house. I sure didn't see that coming. But I haven't missed how quiet it's been around here. I noticed that you stopped doing your morning vocal exercises, and that you don't sing in the shower anymore. And I noticed the way you stopped crunching your food in rhythm to whatever song is in your head, and how you've stopped humming those soft little melodies once you get in bed at night."

I felt like I'd been underwater for a long time and I was fighting my way back to the surface. "You noticed all that?"

"Of course I did," Ma said. "I love you, Tia. And I love listening to you sing more than anything in the entire world. I'd do just about anything to get that back again."

I sat up straighter. "Does this mean you'll let me go see my dad? And maybe you'll come to the fund-raiser if Ms. Marion agrees that the choir can sing?"

"Tia," Ma started, but then she stopped. "I just don't want you to get hurt."

"I know, Ma," I said. "I'm scared too. But maybe if we did things together . . ."

"Together, huh?" Ma laughed a quiet, bitter laugh. "Tia, you have no idea what you're asking."

But she was wrong. I knew exactly what I was asking.

I just wasn't sure Ma had it in her to say yes.

CHAPTER 26

BY THURSDAY afternoon, Ma still hadn't given me an answer about the choir. She'd made some calls about visiting my father, and I supposed that would have to be enough. I'd get to look him in the eyes after eight years and ask him why. Maybe the answer would make things better.

Or maybe it would make things worse.

Ma and I moved around the kitchen like two magnets with the same charge, silently pushing apart even though we wanted to connect. We made our meals and I washed a few dishes, but it was awkward right up until the moment Ma had to leave for work. She stood in the doorway in her store uniform with her purse tucked under her arm. Hovering.

"Are you going to tell Ms. Marion about the invitation tonight?" she asked at last.

I frowned. "Yeah. I won't tell her I'll sing the lead or anything, but . . . the rest of the choir should have a chance to do it, right?"

Ma paused. "Right." She nodded. "Good decision. Smart." She turned as if she were going to leave, but then she stopped again. Her mouth opened and shut as if she'd meant to say something. Finally she said, "You'll be careful walking to the church? Don't talk to strangers and—"

I groaned. "I know, Ma. You say the same thing every time. I think I've got it by now."

Ma walked over and kissed the top of my head. "It's not you I don't trust, it's—"

"People like my father. Uh-huh."

I finally knew how that sentence ended, but Ma's eyes opened wide, as if even now she hadn't expected me to understand. She sucked in a breath, and then forced a thin smile. "Okay, then. Have fun tonight."

I shrugged. Seemed like a long time since anything had been fun. I remembered what Ms. Marion had said that day in my lesson about how some people needed joy in order to create. Was I one of them? Did that mean I might never create anything beautiful again? If I wasn't brave enough to sing for Danielle's family, and I wasn't good enough to sing for the Raven woman, then what was the point?

At that moment, joy seemed impossibly far away.

When the clock hit five, I left my house, locking the door behind me. I followed my usual path, trying to push away the oppressive gray of the sky and the hopeless feeling in my heart. As always, I took the shortcut straight through No Man's-Land.

The temperature was 102, so I had on jean shorts and flip-flops, but as I got nearer, I wished I'd worn long pants despite the heat. I could see the men watching me as I approached, and I willed myself not to turn around.

They were sitting on the steps of the abandoned building drinking beer, just like always, but this time instead of studying my feet, I made myself look at them.

There were five men, three older and two younger, and one of the older ones wore a tropical shirt and a straw hat. They were laughing and joking, tipping back their drinks like they were at a summer barbecue.

"Hey baby," one of the young guys called out. I recognized him immediately. He was the guy who'd aimed his fingers in the shape of a gun. My palms started to sweat, and I almost broke into a run.

"Come on over!" He held out his beer, as if there was even the slightest chance I would take it. But this time, one of the older guys swatted him upside the head.

"Knock it off. Leave that girl alone."

"What?" the young guy said. "Why you messing with my mojo?"

"'Cause you're being a fool as always."

They broke out in a chorus of laughter, but it wasn't at my

expense, and for the first time I wondered if maybe these guys weren't as dangerous as they'd seemed. Don't get me wrong. I wasn't going to stop and chat, but my heart quit pounding out of my chest, and instead of sprinting the rest of the way to church, I kept a steady pace.

Then, just like that, I was off their radar, moving past them, on my own.

∾

For once I was early to choir, and I was surprised that Keisha was too. And Kenny. Seemed odd, since Keisha had dance class right before, and Kenny came straight from practice, but it felt good to walk into the sanctuary and see my two best friends standing side by side, heads together. I knew in my gut they'd showed up early especially for me, just so I'd know they cared.

"Ah!" Ms. Marion said when I joined them. "The third Musketeer has arrived!"

Kenny grinned, and I snuck a glance at Keisha, hoping she was okay with that.

The corner of her mouth quirked up. "Fine," she said. "Guess there's no arguing with Ms. Marion." She was acting put-out, but I could tell she didn't mind adding Kenny to our group.

I went up to Ms. Marion and handed her the yellow flyer.

"I got an invitation for the choir to sing at this fundraiser. I'm not sure I can make it, but I think the choir should do it. It's for . . . Danielle. The girl who . . ." I was pretty sure Ms. Marion knew exactly who Danielle was without my having to explain. "Er . . . the foundation raises money for families who are affected by violence, and Danielle's family organizes this event."

Keisha appeared at my elbow. "They asked Tia to sing the lead on 'I Know.'" She shot eye rays at Mary-Kate, who'd just arrived hand in hand with Khalil. The two of them sat down together in one of the back pews and within seconds they were practically making out. "They specifically asked *Tia* to do it."

"Keisha," I said, "I'm not even sure I'm going to be there."

"You have to go," Keisha said. "Just because your mother won't come, doesn't mean—"

"Girls . . . girls!" Ms. Marion said. "How about I start by contacting the foundation and verifying the invitation? Then we can check the choir's schedule and *then* we'll worry about who will sing the lead."

Keisha scowled, but I couldn't help feeling relieved.

Kenny had come up beside me, and he reached over and took my hand. "You should d-do it, Tia," he said. "Esp-esp . . . especially if they asked for you. That's really amazing."

His hand felt good in mine. Solid and warm.

"I haven't sung in weeks," I said. "I'm not even sure I can sing tonight, let alone at the Mortons' fund-raiser."

"Then let's practice," Keisha said. "I've got music on my phone. Want to sing something?"

I could feel Ms. Marion's eyes on me, waiting for my answer.

"I guess if—"

"Oh my God. Is that your mother?"

Keisha's jaw dropped, and I spun around, completely certain she was wrong. Ma had gone to work. I'd watched her leave.

But there she was, framed in the open doorway.

Parents were arriving with their kids in tow, the preacher man was straightening a pile of papers in the back, old Nana Whiskers was muttering to herself, and Ms. Evette was chasing Jerome around the sanctuary, but all of that activity came to a grinding halt.

Ma was still in her Winn-Dixie uniform. Her face was pale, and she looked like she might turn and run. I knew I ought to go over, but I was too stunned to move.

"Is that her?" someone asked.

"That's the murderer's wife," Mary-Kate whispered to Khalil, loud enough for everyone to hear.

Her words kicked me into gear. "No," I snapped, stomping down the aisle. "That's my mom."

It was as if I'd turned a faucet back on. Ms. Evette hurried to Ma and hugged her, and the preacher man came over to shake Ma's hand. Then Ms. Evette was herding Ma down the center aisle, and I met them halfway.

"What are you doing here?" I sputtered. "You have work tonight."

Ma smiled in a strained way that didn't quite make it to her eyes. Her hands trembled, and she clenched them tight. "I haven't taken a sick day in eight years," she said. "I decided it was time."

"That's . . . I mean, I can't believe . . ." I couldn't tear my eyes away from the sight of Ma here in this church. At my rehearsal. I flung my arms around Ma's middle, not even caring who was watching. "I'm so glad you're here."

"Me too," Ma said.

"Do you want me to sit with you?" I asked, but Ma looked taken aback.

"Of course not. I came to hear you sing."

"I'd be happy to keep your mother company," Ms. Evette said. "Now you kids run along and get some warm-up time before Marion starts rehearsal."

"Come on," Keisha said, tugging at my elbow. "We have five minutes left, and we need to make sure your voice is strong for your mom. Let's sneak downstairs."

Keisha was pushing me forward the way she'd pushed Dwayne that night in the hallway, digging in her heels to make me move, but it was hard to leave when Ma was sitting just a few feet from me, her shoulders stiff and her back straight. Felt as if she might disappear the minute I looked away.

"Your mother is p-pretty," Kenny said. "Like you."

I knew I had a goofy grin spreading from ear to ear, but I couldn't bring myself to care. I followed Keisha and Kenny downstairs and we leaned against the lockers, our feet making a line of V's.

"Ready to give it a try?" Keisha said. "I have the perfect song queued up."

I nodded and she hit the play button on her phone.

I'd been expecting "Amazing Grace" or "A Note to God," but it was "Pyramid," and for some reason that made tears pool in my eyes. I reached over and squeezed Keisha's hand. She was right—"Pyramid" was perfect. I listened for my cue, reaching down to that solid inner core, right where Dwayne had poked me.

Was my music still there?

The first words came out quiet, but crisp and clean, and Keisha hissed, "Yes!"

Even as I sang, I grinned in relief. Breathing deep, I let Charice's voice lead the way, carrying me along until I reached the chorus, and that's when something clicked. I thought about the words I was singing and how Keisha had chosen this song—not only today, but that day when she'd told me the truth about my father. And I thought about what those words meant: *Pyramid, we built this on a solid rock . . .*

I looked at my best friend and knew this was the truth: No matter what else happened in life, I had something unbreakable. My voice soared, and I stood up straight, rolling my shoulders back and drawing the sound from that deep well inside. My song lifted high, power pulsing out of me, louder and louder until I knew they'd hear me upstairs. Down the block. All over New Orleans.

Keisha and Kenny high-fived.

"Sing with me," I said, and they did. Their voices intertwined with mine, Keisha's high soprano augmenting the melody.

And even when the wind is blowing

We'll never fall, just keep on going

Kenny came in on Iyaz's parts, fumbling the words as best he could, but we still sounded good.

Really good.

When the song ended, we all looked at one another and laughed.

Kenny was grinning the same way I'd grinned about my mom, and he looked handsome, so before I could chicken out, I leaned over and kissed him.

"Ewww, gross! No kissing!" Keisha made a disgusted face and gagging noises, but it was still a perfect kiss.

"Wow," Kenny said, and he didn't even stutter.

"Let's sing that again," Keisha said. "We sounded awesome together."

So that's what we did.

Side by side, we sang the lyrics to "Pyramid" as loud as we could, filling our lungs as if our breath were a gift.

And it was.

CHAPTER 27

THAT NIGHT, for the first time, Ma and I walked back from choir rehearsal together. I held her hand and sang the entire way home, one measure at a time, a line of music here, another line there. I replayed the entire rehearsal in my mind, from the brand-new song Ms. Marion had introduced, to the ones we'd been singing for years.

Ms. Marion had let us march around the sanctuary while we sang "When the Saints Go Marching In" as if we were a true New Orleans Second Line. She never usually let us do that since the boys got riled up, but I suspected she'd made an exception because Ma was there, and that made it even more perfect.

As we walked, I was skipping ahead, then falling behind, never letting go of Ma's hand, and she was being dragged back and forth. Ma was pretending to be annoyed, but I could tell she was happy.

"You sounded so good," she kept saying, shaking her

head. “I knew you would, but to hear you sing with a whole choir behind you . . . everything was so loud with the drums and the clapping!” She sighed. “And then when you came in with your part, everyone stopped to listen. Did you see the way that woman in the front row had her eyes closed and her hands in the air the whole time you sang?”

“That was Ms. Jo Jo. She always does that.”

“And the old woman? The one with the—”

“Whiskers?”

Ma and I both laughed.

“Yes. That one. She just lit up when she was listening to you kids sing. At first I thought she seemed kind of crazy, but then I could tell how much she adores all of you.”

“She doesn’t even have a kid in the choir, but she comes to every rehearsal!”

“Really?” Ma said. “She just comes to listen?”

“Uh-huh. Sometimes she brings friends from the old folks’ home.”

Ma shook her head. “I’m so proud of you.”

I grinned. “Thanks, Ma.”

We’d reached our house, and my mother paused on our front steps, keys dangling from her fingers. She inhaled, then let the air out in a loud stream. “You need to sing at the fund-raiser,” she said at last. “I’m sorry I didn’t see it before, but you can make a difference, Tia. You have a real gift.”

I stopped halfway up the front steps, my heart pounding hard. "Do you really think so?"

Ma nodded. "I've always known you were talented, but I've acted like your gift was meant just for me." She paused. "I didn't understand how your singing could touch other people, but I get it now."

Ma reached out and cradled my cheek in the palm of her hand. Her fingers were tough from the calluses she got baking and cleaning at the store, but even with the rough spots, nothing felt as good as Ma's touch.

"Do you think you can do it?" she asked.

A hundred thoughts crowded my head. Thoughts about what it would feel like to meet the Mortons and stand up in front of a crowd, knowing people would see me and think of what my father had done. But then I thought about Keisha and Kenny standing up there with me, and Ma watching in the audience.

"Yes," I said. "I know I can."

"Good," Ma said, "because I spoke to Ms. Marion, and she's going to contact the Morton family. I told her I'd speak to them as well, once we've visited your father." Ma's brows knit together. "Let's get that over with first. One terrifying thing at a time, right?"

"Are you sure?" I asked. "I mean, really, truly sure?"

Ma let out a shrill little laugh. "Do I seem sure about anything?" she asked. "Because if I do, I can guarantee it's an act.

But yes, if this is important to you, then we'll go visit your dad. I asked for the day off on Saturday and I've called the prison to clear our visit."

A shiver ran down my spine despite the heat. *Saturday.* It was sooner than I'd expected. Part of me wanted to hold on to this new feeling of happiness just a little longer. It seemed so fragile, as if life had barely begun knitting back together, and now I was going to tear it apart again.

But I also knew the truth.

My father had done something horrible—the worst thing a person could do—and I needed to understand why that had happened.

CHAPTER 28

SATURDAY MORNING, I woke up feeling as if I hadn't slept at all. It was raining steady, and Ma offered to make us a feast, but I shook my head. There was no use pretending either of us would enjoy it.

I wasn't sure who was more nervous—me or Ma. When we set out, Ma looked pale and she clutched the steering wheel so hard, her knuckles were white. She'd had to ask for a whole day off from work and borrow a car from a coworker, and Ma hated to drive. Plus, I knew she didn't want to see my father, so every time I looked at her, guilt piled up like landfill.

We didn't talk on the way to the prison. Ma kept her eyes fixed on the road, and I stared out the window, watching the countryside pass us by. When Route 66 finally ended at the prison gates, I held my breath, waiting for memories from my last visit to flood back in.

They didn't. Everything felt new, from the huge property

with the surrounding barbed-wire fences, to the posts with armed guards looming above us. The prison was right on the Mississippi River, lush greenery dipping into babbling water, while men with guns kept watch in towers overhead.

Ma and I stood in line to get checked in as guards with dogs circled the area. We had to go through a metal detector and get patted down and then take a prison bus to the right building. Ma had warned me not to wear any jewelry and to choose clothes that were plain, so I'd opted for jeans, sneakers, and a green T-shirt, and I'd worn my hair down instead of pulled back so that my hair clip wouldn't set off the metal detector.

When we finally got to the visiting room, Ma reached over and took my hand. The room was large and crowded with inmates and families, talking and eating together. I couldn't imagine eating anything, and the smell of fried chicken and catfish made my stomach cramp.

"Will they bring him in soon?" I asked, glancing at the door.

"Yes," Ma said, studying my face. "Are you okay?"

I nodded, but I could hardly breathe.

"Did he want to see me?" I'd been avoiding that question, but now I wondered if my father might not show up.

Ma paused. "I don't know how your father feels about things," she said, "but he agreed to meet with us."

I remembered when my father had said not to bring me

here, and I couldn't stop my knees from shaking under the table. Then Ma nodded toward the door, and there he was being led in by a guard.

After all these years, he looked almost the same as I'd remembered. Maybe he was thinner, but mostly he had all the same lines and angles as before. His eyes were still dark and deep set, his arms thick and strong. Seemed strange that I ever could have forgotten him.

He walked slowly toward our table, staring right at me.

"Tia?" he said at last, as if he wasn't entirely sure.

I nodded and we gaped at each other like the strangers that we were.

I swallowed hard, but my throat was completely dry. My father shifted from one foot to the other, and then he looked at my mother. There was such a mixture of pain and love in his gaze that I wanted to look away, but I couldn't.

"Baby?" he whispered, his voice cracking.

My mother's eyes welled up. "Lyle," she breathed.

Then we were silent again for far too long, until finally my father sat down across from us. "How you been?" he said at last, but it wasn't clear who he was asking, so I waited for Ma to answer. When she didn't, I guessed she was leaving the talking up to me.

"Okay," I said.

"You've gotten real big," my father murmured, "and pretty. You look like your mama." I didn't, so I wondered if he really thought that or if he was just saying it. Then he turned to Ma. "You look good too."

My mother held every part of herself completely still.

"Thank you."

My mind screamed, *This was a mistake!* But despite everything, another part of me wished he'd reach out and hold my hand. How could I want that?

I opened my mouth, praying that words would come out. "Thanks for seeing me," I said at last.

My father laughed, a nervous guffaw. "I was surprised you wanted to come."

"Me too," I said. "I guess... I needed to ask you some things."

This was harder than I'd ever imagined.

"You're twelve now," my father said. "I should've expected as much."

It was as close as we'd come to acknowledging why he was in here.

My palms were starting to sweat, and I shut my eyes tight, just for an instant. "I wondered if you're sorry," I said, blurting the words out. "And I wanted to know why you did it."

My mother's jaw fell open and she reached over to take my arm. Even the people sitting nearby were staring.

"Tia," Ma started, but my father held up one bony hand.

"It's okay," he said. "She has a right to ask."

He scratched the dark stubble on his chin, and for one eternal moment, I waited.

"Yeah," he said, at last. "I'm sorry. And I know you probably came here wanting me to say it was an accident or something, but I made up my mind I'm not going to lie to you about any of it."

It felt so good to hear that word—*sorry*—come out of his mouth, but I knew it wasn't enough. "If you're sorry, then how could you do it in the first place?"

My father paused. He glanced at Ma, then back at me. "I don't know," he said. "I ask myself that a whole lot, and maybe I'm just a real bad person. Alls I know is, I was drunk, and I was in that house to steal some money, and that girl came out and surprised me, and it happened in a split second.

"I had my gun, and I saw her standing there in her pajamas, and I thought, 'Lyle, that girl is going to call the police and she knows just what you look like.' Then my finger pulled the trigger before I thought anything else. I wish I would've thought it through some more, but I didn't. And some things . . . you can't take 'em back."

There it was. The truth from my father's own mouth.

My breath hitched hard.

"Bad enough what I done to that girl," my father said, "but then I went and left you and your ma all alone. Figured you were better off without me, so I never wrote or nothing, but when your ma called . . . well, I know I don't deserve this visit."

He was looking at me, begging me with his eyes not to hate him. I thought of Danielle and her family, the baby and everyone who loved him. I even thought about Keisha. For every one of their sakes I should have stood up and left now that I'd gotten what I came for, but instead I sat there studying the features of my father's face. Soaking him in.

This time, I was looking for the good, not the bad.

"So you made a horrible decision?"

Seemed impossible that the reason *why* could get boiled down to something so small. That so many lives could be affected by a split-second wrong choice.

My father leaned back. "No," he said. "It was a whole bunch of stupid decisions one right after another. Shouldn't have been drinking, shouldn't have been in that house, and shouldn't have had my gun. Shouldn't have bought the damn thing in the first place and the kicker is, I bought it for protection after that house near us got robbed. But see, that's what gived me the idea. I knew those people from work and when that Morton guy won all my money in a poker game, I thought, if someone else can do it, and they ain't even got a right to the money, then why can't I do it when it's my money in the first place? You see?"

I didn't, but I nodded.

"Just so's you know," my father said, "I'd been going to write to you someday, even if you hadn't called, and what I wanted to say is that I never deserved your mama." He looked straight at Ma. "She was always too good for me, and even though I never got to know you all that well on account of you being real small when I got put away, I already knew you were gonna turn out more like her than me. And that's a good thing."

Beside me, Ma was crying silently. Then my father said something I never expected in a million years.

"'Bout two years ago," he said, "the Morton family came up here to tell me they forgave me for what I done to them. They'd asked me to go through this program with them that their foundation runs, so we could meet face-to-face and I could say how sorry I am, and they could say they hoped I was saved, and ever since then I've wanted to tell you both that I wished I never hurt you."

My father stopped abruptly. He pinched the bridge of his nose with his fingertips and screwed his mouth up tight. He coughed, then cleared his throat. "That meant something powerful to me," he continued. "Them coming here and all, and I didn't figure you two wanted to hear from me, but I made a promise to myself that if I ever got the chance, I'd say I regret what I done and I wish I could have been a good daddy for you and the right kind of husband for your mama."

My father's final words came out quiet. "I don't expect you to forgive me or anything, but if you ever want to come back and see me again, I'd like to ask you about school and friends and if you still sing songs like you used to when you were small. And . . . I guess that's all I have to say."

Amen.

My mind was swimming. Tears pooled behind my eyes, but I blinked them away. Then Ma stood up and patted my shoulder.

"Give Tia some time to think, Lyle," she said. "This was plenty for today."

My father nodded, and the way he looked at me was heavy, as if there was so much more he wanted to say. He glanced over and signaled to the guard.

"Be good," he said, standing up, and then he looked at Ma. The two of them stared deep into each other's eyes as if they were having a whole conversation. Then my father started to walk away, but I stood up quick.

"Wait!"

The guard stopped, and my father turned. Before I could lose my courage, I ran over and threw my arms around him. At first, he just stood there, but then, slowly, his arms wrapped around me. I heard his heart beat, and his embrace felt strong and safe. It shouldn't have, but it did. I breathed in the scent of him and held on tight until the guard made me let go.

CHAPTER 29

ON THE DRIVE home, I sat beside Ma in silence, feeling light-headed, my brain overwhelmed. I hadn't eaten since the night before, and my insides were tied in knots. Ma stared at the road ahead as if it might disappear if her eyes strayed for even a second. Her knuckles were white on the steering wheel, and I knew—*just knew*—that every inch of her wanted to howl.

I felt a stab in my gut and clutched at the door handle.

"Ma?"

"*What?*" It came out meaner than she'd probably meant it.

I swallowed hard. "Could we stop at the rest area up ahead?"

Ma took in a shaky breath, then nodded. "Sorry I snapped at you. I guess I'm still a little tense."

She got off at the rest stop exit, pulled the car over, and I leaped out, pausing a second to get my bearings before jogging over to the women's room while Ma waited in the car. The rest area was small and dirty, as if no one remembered it was there. The bathroom smelled the way bathrooms do when it's hot out and no one cleans them, and the odor made me want to gag, but I slipped into a stall.

When I sat down, my breath caught. I'd gotten my period. Relief mingled with pain. All that waiting and it had finally happened. Today of all days.

I left the stall and ran back out to the car. Ma's window was already open, and she peered out at me.

"I got my period, Ma," I said, breathless.

Ma shrugged. "It's not unusual to have it again so soon. Girls your age can be irregular when they first start." She rustled some quarters from the depths of her frayed purse. "Here's some money for the machine. From now on, carry supplies with you all the time, just in case."

The quarters felt cold and heavy in my hand. I wanted more from her, but I knew this was all I'd get. And that was my own fault. "Okay," I said. "I will."

I jogged back to the restroom and stood by myself, thinking about the way I'd once believed this moment would transform me into a woman. As if one day I'd be a little girl, and the next I'd be all grown up.

Now I understood. There was nothing simple about

this transformation. No caterpillar bursting forth from the cocoon with beautiful, delicate wings, ready to soar across the open sky. That was the myth, but the truth was something different: messy, confusing, and full of mistakes.

But the truth was all I had.

CHAPTER 30

THE MORNING of the fund-raiser came up quicker than I thought. Ma was true to her word. She and Ms. Marion had been in touch with the Mortons, and they'd gone over to the foundation together to work out all the details of the Rainbow Choir's performance. The meeting had lasted for three hours, and Ma said they'd been hard but good ones—that they'd talked about what my father did, and the pain of the trial, and all the long years afterward. She said in the end, Mr. Morton had hugged her, and Mrs. Morton had smiled, and she'd looked so much like Danielle's picture that Ma had cried.

"I made a right fool of myself, standing there bawling in the foundation boardroom," Ma told me. "Thank goodness Marion was there. It was good of her to go with me."

I'd wanted to go too, but Ma had been hard as iron again.

You do not need to apologize, Tia Rose. I won't hear of it. Not a single speck of what happened was your fault. You hear me? Don't let me catch you dwelling on things that are not your responsibility.

The words had been familiar, but there had been something different when she'd said them. She'd reminded me of those pointed black fences in the Garden District, the way they protected what was theirs without hiding the beautiful mansions and colorful flowers behind their bars.

"Did they tell you why they invited me to sing?" I'd asked. It was the one question I still hadn't been able to answer.

Ma had shifted her weight from one foot to the other, and I'd known she wasn't entirely comfortable with what they'd had to say.

"Yes," she'd said. "They told me we're all victims of Lyle's violence. You and me, Tia. Not just them." Ma had shaken her head. "Seems too generous. But if you can do something to help them out by singing at their fund-raiser, and if I finally got up the courage to say I'm sorry after eight long years . . . well, I guess that's the best we can do, isn't it?"

I agreed. Mostly.

There was no doubt in my mind that I'd sing my heart out at the fund-raiser. I had the lead on 'I Know,' plus I was singing 'Pyramid' with Keisha and Kenny. We'd been practicing every day for the past week, even going in for extra lessons with Ms. Marion to set up the arrangement. Every time we sang together, our harmony got tighter. Now when I thought about performing in front of the Mortons, my heart still pounded, but it was a mixed feeling—part nervousness and part excitement.

I also knew that the Mortons having the courage to invite me would make an impression on everyone who heard me sing.

And that was an amazing opportunity, wasn't it?

So why did I feel like there was an important piece of the puzzle still missing?

Maybe the most important piece of all.

~

That morning it was overcast, and I walked slowly, taking my time and feeling the rhythm in my feet as my sneakers slapped against the concrete of the sidewalk. The worst of the heat wave that had swamped New Orleans for the past weeks had moved on, and now the air was cooler, but the sky was still heavy and gray.

When I got to the baby's house, I stopped. The memorial fence was gone, and someone had swept the sidewalk clean. I wondered what had happened to the teddy bears and candles, the poems and pictures.

What had happened to my father's photo?

My chest clenched with a pang of loss, but I kept going, inside the gate and up the steps until I reached the front door and rang the bell.

I didn't expect an answer. I waited a moment, then

slipped the flyer for the fund-raiser in the mailbox. I'd written a note on top saying that I hoped their family would come, and I'd included the foundation's phone number in case they couldn't make it. I wasn't entirely sure if they would be able to read my note, but I had to try.

As soon as I let the flyer go, I turned to leave, but then the door opened, and there she was, tall and beautiful, wearing a long patchwork skirt that had tiny silver bells at the bottom hem line.

"Hello," she said, her dark eyes searching mine.

I chewed on my bottom lip. "Hi."

She held up one long, delicate finger. "Wait," she told me. Then she disappeared inside the house, and when she returned, she was holding the photograph of my father.

"Yours, yes?"

She handed it to me, and the photo felt smooth against my fingers. "Yes," I said. "My father." I traced the lines of his face with the pad of my thumb.

"Ahhh." We stood in silence for a moment, but it wasn't uncomfortable. "Sit?" she asked at last.

"Okay," I said, sitting down on the steps. She sat beside me, one step up. Her skirt made a tinkling sound as she moved.

"Braid?" she asked, reaching out to touch my hair with gentle fingers.

I smiled, surprised. "Yes, please."

Then she stroked my forehead, forming strands, and twisting each one carefully, intertwining all the pieces.

"What is . . ." She frowned. "Name," she said at last.

"Tia," I said.

"Aa'ida."

I repeated the syllables after her, slowly and carefully. "Ah-ee-da?" I turned around to make sure I'd gotten it right.

She nodded and her dark spiraling hair fell over her shoulder. She reached into her shirt and pulled out a small locket. When she opened it, I recognized the baby's photo with his sweet, toothy smile.

"Aksander."

I ran my finger over the baby's face.

"Ak-zan-der," I repeated. "He's beautiful," I added, and—Aa'ida's eyes filled with tears.

"Love of mine," she said. "Always."

She said the word *always* so that it sounded like two words.

All ways.

"You come see me," Aa'ida said. "Some . . . times. O-K?"

"Okay," I said, closing my eyes against the gentle tug of her hands. "I'd like that."

"Is good to see . . . child."

I wasn't sure if she meant me or children in general, but it didn't matter. I'd visit as often as I could even if all I ever did was sit on the front step to get my hair braided. Maybe I'd ask her about Aksander and I'd listen the way Kenny had listened to me, without trying to make things better.

We were quiet for a long time, and then Aa'ida began to hum as she worked her long fingers through the tangles in my hair. She wove a French braid, then two smaller braids on the sides, but each time she let the strands fall and began all over again. Felt good. When she started to sing softly—lines of unfamiliar music in minor keys—I hummed along.

The sky grew darker, but it didn't rain. The air was still. The streets were quiet save for Aa'ida's voice. Sometimes, I sang a line after her, fumbling over the strange words, and she'd nod and sing the line again more slowly, so I could repeat it. Once I'd learned a certain line, she'd add the harmony while I sang the melody. Then we sang together, two quiet voices pushing away the darkness.

It was more than I'd hoped for.

It was enough.

∾

AUTHOR'S NOTE

Dear Reader,

As an author, one of the questions I get asked most often is whether my books are based on real events. Are the characters similar to people I know? Did the idea for the plot come from something that happened in my own life? Are my main character and I alike?

Every book is different, but the answer is always the same. All of my writing is infused with real life. While no character, place, or event is ever an exact replication, the heart of a story comes from things that have meaning to me.

Like Tia, I once sang in a gospel choir. I also lived in New Orleans for a time and fell in love with that beautiful city and all its color, flavor, and music. But most important, like Tia, I struggle with the question of why bad things happen. Even as a young girl, I wanted answers. My parents tried hard to protect me from the tough parts of life, but I still heard about what was happening on the news. I still lost a friend in the fourth grade who passed away too young. And years later, like Tia, I still heard the gunshots that killed a child.

Now I'm a mother, and even though I sometimes wish my son could grow up in a great big bubble where nothing bad ever happens, I also know that as he grows older, he'll have to face his own struggles, heartaches, fears, and challenges. So, what I *truly* wish is that he'll feel love surrounding him even when life is hardest. I hope he'll know that it's okay to question why and even if the answers aren't as simple as he'd like, he'll know he's not alone in asking tough questions. I hope that, like Tia, struggling with the hard stuff will help him find strength, give him empathy, and help him feel more connected to the people around him who might be struggling too.

I wish these same things for you, my wonderful reader. No matter what's happening in your life, remember that connecting to people you trust can make you stronger. Whether it's a parent, sibling, friend, teacher, or guidance counselor, there are others who can help you through difficult times. And like Tia, I hope you'll find lots of love, hope, and joy in the end.

Peace,

K L Going

ACKNOWLEDGMENTS

There is so much to be said about the process of writing this novel, which was an emotional journey from start to finish. I have depended greatly on the patience and grace of my editor, Kathy Dawson, as well as her incredible skill. I'm also indebted to my amazing agent, Ginger Knowlton, who buoyed me up each time I thought I couldn't go any farther. You both have my infinite gratitude for not giving up on this book.

A story that takes four years to write doesn't happen without the tremendous sacrifice of one's family. Thank you to the two loves of my life, Dustin Adams and Ashton Adams. I adore you.

To Brenda Zook Friesen, Suzanne Southard, and Julie Litwiller-Shank: our time in New Orleans infused every page of this book. I can't imagine my life's journey without you. Thank you as well to my parents, William and Linda Going. My father's involvement with prison ministry was an inspiration to create a balanced portrayal of Tia's father.

I hope I've succeeded. Thanks to my grandmother Jillian Bedard, who provided her expertise in speech therapy, and to Donna Jones, who (way back in college!) asked me to join *The Angels of Harmony* and encouraged me to share my voice. Thanks to Marileta Robinson, Clara Gillow Clark, Claire Evans, Regina Castillo, and so many others who read drafts of this novel and gave me their valuable feedback. I'd also like to thank The Port Jervis Free Library and The Highlights Foundation, who provided me with quiet space to write.

Finally, I'm so grateful to the parents, grandparents, teachers, librarians, and mentors who share my books with kids. It's not easy to help children deal with the tough parts of life, but it's essential, because in the end, there aren't any answers to why, only the circle of love and support we create as we ask the question.